I'm in the
Room

Lawrence Weill

UNIVERSITY *of*
NORTH GEORGIA
UNIVERSITY PRESS

Dahlonega, GA

Copyright © by Lawrence Weill

All rights reserved. No part of this book may be reproduced in whole or in part without written permission from the publisher, except by reviewers who may quote brief excerpts in connections with a review in newspaper, magazine, or electronic publications; nor may any part of this book be reproduced, stored in a retrieval system, or transmitted in any form or by any means electronic, mechanical, photocopying, recording, or other, without the written permission from the publisher.

Published by:
University of North Georgia Press
Dahlonega, Georgia

Printing Support by:
Lightning Source Inc.
La Vergne, Tennessee

Cover Photo: "The Out There Chair"
Photographer: Flabber DeGasky
Cover Photo License: CC BY 2.0

Book Cover Design by Corey Parson

Layout by Amy Beard

ISBN: 978-1-940771-24-3

Table of Contents

Prologue — vii

I	Thesis	9
II	Abstract Qualities	17
III	Shape and Quantity	22
IV	Measure	32
V	Quality	38
VI	Substance and Accident	47
VII	Cause and Effect	57
VIII	Reciprocity	68
IX	Essence	75
X	Subjective Notion	80
XI	Objective Notion	87
XII	Evolution	95
XIII	Revolution	102
XIV	Devolution	112
XV	The Crucible	130

Epilogue — 141

For Jennie

Prologue

Nothing is so common-place as to wish to be remarkable.
-Oliver Wendell Holmes, Sr.,
The Autocrat of the Breakfast Table (1858), Ch. XII

It is an oddity of life that a person can never completely know one's self because, even if it were possible to completely define a person, just the act of defining that person would change the definition. The only possible way, then, to know about people is to try to see who they are becoming rather than who they are. But if we want to see who they are becoming, we must see who they were, for the act of becoming presupposes being. You must already be someone in order to become someone (or something) else. Such is the case of Allen Johnson whom no one saw—or at least rarely saw. It wasn't that he was invisible, but simply that he was not very visible. The people around him, indeed, the world in general was not interested in seeing him. What he did not realize for a good deal of his life was that his understanding of his lack of visibility would eventually set him free. To be unknown is liberating. But he did not always know that; in fact, he could not have known that until the circumstances allowed the assorted variables in his life to bring that understanding to him. First, the fact of his being had to manifest itself. The abstract external characteristics of his life had to be established. Then he would need to align his own stars to be able to determine his fate.

Thesis

To be fit for life in society every child, as well as every dog, must be housebroken.
                                                                -Edwin G. Conklin

It's not clear when Allen Johnson discovered that no one saw him, but certainly he had seen the possibility coming long before it happened. Perhaps he only really knew how invisible he might be two months after he turned thirty-one. That was when he made the Flying Leap, as he later described it when he told tales of life to his nearly-invisible children and then later to his mostly-invisible grandchildren. But that Flying Leap wasn't until well after he had started down the path to anonymity and had placed that invisibility in opposition to the prominence he dreamed of as a child and then as a young man. Allen Johnson alternately struggled against his obscurity and reveled in it, so he was ever engaged in a kind of bittersweet dialectic. And eventually, as with all dialectics, he found himself in a position of self-revolution and then complete devolution. At that point, Allen Johnson made the Flying Leap. But in the meanwhile, he developed every sort of sometimes ingenious, sometimes absurd scheme to overcome his hiddenness.

It's important to realize that Allen Johnson had not always been turning invisible. For most of his life, he wavered somewhere between perceptible and imperceptible, and his numerous strategies for overcoming his obscurity were generally predicated on the basis of volume and color. This is certainly true of his early years. Born one bright May morning in the late fifties, he was a mostly-distinguishable baby and was destined to grow up in Evanston, a town in the western end of Kentucky that was mostly unknown to the outside world, despite being the self-proclaimed corn-on-the-cob center of the universe.

With this proclamation came a yearly celebration of corn with the ever popular ear toss and coronation of the Cob Queen, a title highly coveted by the cheerleaders and pom-pom girls at Evanston Senior High School. Unfortunately the winner, who wore the genuine gold-colored tiara with rows of corn designed, etched, and painstakingly assembled at Goldberg's Trophy House, Pawn Shop, and Bait Store, was obligated to relinquish the tiara to the new Cob Queen the following year. But that did not dissuade the young ladies from entering the contest, as they were also determined to shine forth from the shadows of insignificance and ride in the convertible supplied by Jimmy Jones Ford in the annual Corn-on-the-Cob Parade.

Even as a baby, Allen Johnson tried diligently to be perceived in this town of which so few from outside were even aware. Allen threw up quite often colorful, viscous baby food and managed to drool on anyone who picked him up, traits that clearly made people notice. Early on, he discovered he could see his own hand and could even shove it into his mouth, and if his parents—youthful, eager, and naive—did not notice him, he had a plan to remedy that. He would let out a highly audible yowl that caused dogs in the neighborhood to cringe and guaranteed that his parents and other sentient creatures were aware of his existence.

Yet even then, despite his precocious volume, despite his very existence as a flesh and blood baby, sometimes Allen's own mother, Jean, just didn't see him. A romantic movie (she was especially fond of Doris Day movies) would show on the Afternoon Matinee, and she would get caught up in it, completely missing the obvious fact that Allen was there and demanded constant attention (like all children until the age of twenty-five). He used his trusty tool, the 120 decibel yowl, but if it was during the Dialing for Dollars segment, his mother didn't see or hear him and went on watching the movie until Doris fell in love with the scoundrel she had treated like the plague for an hour and a half. It was as if Jean was certain the answer to her family's occasional financial woes would be remedied by a random call from the television station.

"And now it's time to call today's lucky viewer . . ."

"Aiyeeee!" Allen howled, his diaper uncomfortably heavy and wet. The family cat scampered into the farthest reaches of the house.

"Hush, Allen, Bob Bolger might be trying to call us."

"Today's number is in the Rosemont area . . ."

"Oh, that's where Carol lives. I wonder if he's calling Carol."

"Aiyeeeee!" Both the pitch and the volume increased. Neighbors a block away looked up from their newspapers curiously.

"The first three digits are five, three, six . . ."

"Oh, that's the same as Carol's number."

"Aiyeeeeeee!" Allen's face bulged red with effort. Birds stopped flying over the house.

"What if she doesn't know the secret clue? I'd feel awful if she didn't know the secret clue and Bob Bolger called her."

"Aiyeeeee!"

Whirrr, whirrr, whirrr. "Carol?"

"Aiyeeeee! Aiyeee!" Other children in their homes joined in the chorus, their mothers perplexed by the sudden outbursts.

"Carol, are you watching the movie on channel seven? You are? Great!"

"Aaaah! Waaaah! Aiyeeeee!" Allen's eyes bugged out with effort now.

"We're dialing the last of the number now . . ."

"Well, I'd better get off so Bob can reach you if he's calling your number."

"Aaaaah aaaaah haaaaah! Aiyeee!" The windows rattled now.

"What? What did you say Carol? I'm sorry, but the baby's—"

"Waaaah!" Paint began to buckle along the wall.

"Hush up, honey. What? Oh, okay, bye."

Bob Bolger shook his head as he hung up the phone. "Well, our number was busy, so the pot for tomorrow goes up ten dollars to three hundred twenty dollars."

"Aiyeeee!"

"Well, I guess it was somebody else's number."

"And now back to Pillow Talk."

"Aiyeeee!"

Somewhere down the street, a dachshund cried mournfully. "Oooooooh. Yipe, yipe, ooooooooh."

His father, Roger, who had handed out the stale cigars with "It's a Boy!" printed on them to all of his friends; who had bounced Allen on his knee until he vomited (Allen, that is, although sometimes that made his father gag as well); who had promised Allen before he could see that Allen would be the shortstop he himself had always wanted to be; sometimes seemed incapable of seeing Allen. Roger Johnson would pull the Valiant into the drive after driving home from the Motor Pool Division of Northwestern Kentucky Electric Corp. where he was the Assistant Dispatch Manager Trainee, and Allen would hear the familiar ping of the engine and make himself as visible as possible, usually by spurting forth a whitish liquid. But when Mr. Johnson came in, his necktie pulled loose and his jacket over his arm, he sometimes didn't see the boy he was certain would be an All-American shortstop. Instead, Roger would plop himself into a tattered wingback chair and call to Allen's mother.

"Jean. I'm home."

"Yes, dear. What would you like for dinner?" (Although, dinner usually was well under way.)

"I don't care. I'm too tired to think. I'm exhausted." Then he would drop his heavy arms loudly on the arms of the chair. All of this, of course, was a cue for his wife, and she almost never failed to get it.

"I'm coming." And she would hand him a can of Falls City beer that would somehow revive him and made his breath both sour and sickly sweet. Jean would rub his neck and shoulders. Then his eyes would adjust, and he would finally be able to see Allen. He would walk heavily over to the playpen and smile, his eyes looking tired and puffy in Allen's face.

"Here's my big boy." His eyes softened with affection.

"Aah!" Allen cooed back.

"Did you have a good day, little Ken Boyer?" Roger leaned closer and picked up Allen, holding his son above his head now to look up at him. Allen smiled back, caught a whiff of his father's breath, gasped for fresh air, and vomited.

When he was a baby, Allen's aunts and uncles saw him quite well. They goo-gooed and made faces at him; he watched them with a mixture of amusement and horror. Their faces were funny enough to look at, but the notion that these odd-looking folks with contorted mouths and exaggerated eyes were related to Allen by blood frightened him terribly. If he could have been overlooked by his Aunt Gertie, he would have gladly, but when Allen was a baby, Aunt Gertie always saw him. Despite the fact that being seen was Allen's single mission in life at the time, he could never forget the image of her face very close in his, her eyes bugging out toward him and her saying, "Hesa bitty baby! Yes, hesa bitty baby! Uh huh, he is. Hesa bitty baby!" It was not something Allen or any child got over easily. In fact, for the rest of his life, he always had a certain ambivalence for his parents' siblings and their children.

Allen's grandpa always saw him, and Allen loved that. Allen always felt safe and loved unequivocally around his grandpa. Grandpa was a stoic, practical man who bounced Allen gently on his knee and said things like, "It doesn't matter how you find it out; it only matters that you know what you know." But Grandpa lived in Ohio somewhere, and Allen didn't get to be seen by Grandpa as much as he would have liked. And his other grandfather, known affectionately as Grandfather, was already very old when Allen was born. Besides, he had some fifteen other grandchildren, so he never saw what the big deal was about yet another squalling kid.

He always acted as if Allen wasn't there. And only once did Allen try the yowling routine, because when he did, his grandfather practically threw Allen and his parents out into the street.

"Don't bring that damn Chihuahua back until you get a muzzle on it," and Grandfather slammed the door. At the time, Allen's feelings were hurt, and his parents were angry. But once Allen chose to take the Flying Leap, none of that mattered.

When Allen was five, his parents made him even more unknown, or at least it seemed so to him; they had another child whom they fussed over and carried on about as if they had never before seen a baby (and Allen knew they had. They had seen the perfect baby: him). They named Allen's new sister Darlene after someone's great aunt, and she immediately became the focus of their lives, or so it seemed to Allen. If they ever did see Allen, it was to have him hold the baby so they could take a picture. And when the picture came back, the focus was always on Darlene, and they didn't even care that you couldn't see Allen in the picture. They would ooh and ahh over the picture as if Allen's face wasn't blurry or even sliced off at the nose. As long as "the princess" could be seen, nothing else mattered.

Allen did not like the lack of attention that came as a result of Darlene, and he took a two-pronged approach to remedy the situation. He decided on the one hand that his parents must notice him at any cost. If he could make that happen at the same time that he made his sister unhappy, so much the better. Nearly burning down the house by placing all of the baby's toys in the oven and putting it on broil was a small price to pay for finally getting some attention, although the whipping he received seemed a greater price perhaps. On the other hand, he decided that part of the problem stemmed from the fact that his parents, for some reason, thought Darlene was cute. (He honestly didn't see it. And she couldn't catch a baseball, even when he threw it directly at her face.) He sought to remedy his parents' misperception, first by painting Darlene's face various colors with permanent magic marker, then by cutting off her hair once she grew some. Again, the whipping no doubt was a great price to pay, but at least his father had to see him to whip him.

Even Aunt Gertie couldn't see Allen if Darlene was around. She walked right past him, grabbed the baby, bugged her eyes out and said, "Shesa bitty durl! Uh huh, she is. Shesa bitty durl! Uh huh!" It never occurred to Allen that being jealous of the consideration Aunt Gertie gave Darlene made no sense, since he generally avoided Aunt Gertie's attention. (She had developed the disgusting habit of kissing him, and she wanted him to kiss her back!) No, having a baby sister was not to Allen's liking. But they had not sought Allen's opinion. Had they, he would have told them to forget it, to forget the whole concept of a little sister. But they had not asked.

When he was eleven, he was like all boys, preoccupied by the concept of his own conspicuousness; he balanced precariously between seen and unseen. He wanted to be noticed by a variety of folks. He played catch against a wall with an old tennis ball behind his family's house on Saint Ann Street with the fervent hope (and belief) that Red Schoendienst from the St. Louis Cardinals lurked about the neighborhood. Red would witness his dexterity and remarkable ability to throw out the league's fastest runners streaking for first; surely a contract would arrive in the mail any day now. In his daydreams, which he learned to nurture at an early age, Allen was the surprise starting pitcher for the Cardinals, the first rookie to pitch a no-hitter in his opening game (at eleven!). He also went four for four at the plate (each one a homer) and finally was deliberately walked in the last inning, after which he promptly stole second, third, and home. The hero's parade in Evanston shamed the Corn-on-the-Cob Parade.

Also about this time, Allen began to eagerly seek for the attention of the little girl around the corner on Parrish Avenue, Karen Dobroski. He walked slowly in front of her house, sometimes kicking at a stick or a can, trying to see if she was peeking out the window at him (she wasn't) without being caught looking.

Yet he was, at other times, mortified by the thought of someone looking at him. If his parents gazed at him, motherly or fatherly love cleansing all vision, he would shoot a look back and bark, "What?" If he had to walk across a crowded room, he would hang his head and scuffle across the floor so that no one would notice him (which, of course, they did, because he was shuffling across the floor as if he had some strange ailment that curved his head and spine and prevented him from lifting his feet). It was also about this time that Allen began to understand how to sometimes control his perceptibility. He used that knowledge to his own gain, meager though that gain might be. Once, for instance, he had walked inconspicuously into the Ben Franklin five and dime and managed to shove a whole box of cherry cordial candies under his shirt. He sauntered out nonchalantly and then sprinted to the corner where his trusty Stingray bike with the banana seat stood at the ready in the rack next to the drug store. He pulled the contraband from under his shirt and pedaled off down the street to his best friend Joey's house where Allen proceeded to eat the entire box of candy. He had made himself invisible for just long enough to become a petty thief and then had become miserably ill as a result.

Of course, Allen didn't realize that his father, in spite of his advancing years (what was he, thirty-two? Thirty-three? He was definitely middle aged to Allen's way of thinking), had many of the same struggles. But he had his own avenues for maintaining his sense of self, of imposing his own kind of order on a chaotic and unfeeling universe. For example, Allen's dad had, for many years, collected small boxes and horded little odd-shaped bottles and jars. He kept them and filled them with various tiny objects that otherwise lay around in drawers, jumbled and tangled together. He had one box that had come originally with a Christmas ornament but was now filled with thumbtacks. A jar, aromatic from maraschino cherries, held a lifetime supply of those little add-on erasers that go on the end of pencils Another jar, stained slightly with pickle juice, kept any size machine bolt ever needed handy, but no wood screws were in that jar. Allen's dad certainly would not have wood screws or even hex nuts in with the machine bolts. Everything had its own container.

Sometimes Allen ventured into the basement where his dad's cache of containers lined the shelves along one shadowy concrete wall. Those with screw-on lids attached to the shelf above by virtue of a nail through the top that held tight the accumulation of tiny finishing nails and cotter pins. It was exhilarating just to be there, for this was his father's special place to repair small appliances and various broken toys and furniture. The place had a magical feel; items went in damaged and came out whole.

Dad's collection of containers sat in careful disarray. There was no order to the system of which box went next to which jar as far as Allen could tell. But they stood neatly at the ready at the back edge of the shelves, facing the front if they had a face, or hanging from the pine board above. The sight of them filled Allen with a sense of pride and envy, at least when he was a young boy. He was glad the Johnson family had this unending supply of brass brads and paper clips. Nobody else Allen knew had such a collection, at least to his knowledge. But Allen was also jealous of the splendor of all those little containers. He too could have found some nails, and where would he have put them? Didn't he have those marbles that needed sorting? And then there were his little metal cars and trucks that really could have used some order if only he had one of the cigar boxes that now held a collection of rolls of tape. But Allen did not have the collection of organizers that his dad had. Allen might have started his own collection of jars and boxes, but for some reason his dad seemed to have dibs on the really good ones. It really was unfair. Perhaps his dad's toys were, by definition, more important than Allen's. As a result, they made his father more important, ergo, more visible than Allen. In that sense, even his dad's jars and boxes in the basement made Allen imperceptible.

Allen decided at one point that the futility of his entire life was a vast conspiracy being carried out by everyone in his known world. Everyone in Evanston, including his parents, his teachers, his friends, even his little sister, had surely been selected carefully by the government, perhaps even the United Nations, to perpetrate an elaborate scheme wherein Allen Johnson was to be henceforth unknown beyond the confines of Kingfisher Lake, the farthest reach of Evanston in Allen's experience. Perhaps it was because, in actuality, he had some amazing ability that no one else did, and the government wanted to prevent his finding it out for fear he would exact some terrible calamity on the country, indeed, the planet. It explained why his major league contract hadn't arrived yet; they couldn't allow Allen Johnson out of Evanston because he just might discover the secret about himself that was being maintained. Sometimes Allen pondered on just what that power might be. He knew it wasn't the ability to move objects with his mind; he had tried that and been unsuccessful (although he had managed to develop a massive headache). He also discovered that it wasn't the ability to fly; that resulted in a minor fracture in the arm (really nothing a cast wouldn't remedy). Whatever the secret, they were doing a good job keeping it from him and keeping him hidden from sight. When his family began taking vacations, first to various campgrounds in the Midwest, then to cities like St. Louis and Chicago, Allen's theory ran into considerable difficulty. It was conceivable that the other campers had been screened by the government, but an entire stadium of Cardinals fans? How could they keep from staring at the superhuman in their midst? In the end, Allen abandoned his theory for the much more obvious and plausible answer. No one said anything, no one let out the secret, and no one stared at Allen Johnson because he was, despite his greatest efforts throughout his childhood, completely unremarkable.

Abstract Qualities

Too much youth, in short, is a bore, since youth lacks variety and has little to fall back upon but animal spirits, which are an even greater bore.
                                                                -George Jean Nathan

Of course, Allen wasn't completely imperceptible. He had shape and color and, if he stood in front of the television while the television program *The FBI* was on, Roger (as Allen liked to call his dad at times when he became a teen) would grumble something about his being a better door than window, and Allen would begrudgingly move to the side. And Allen himself was aware that he wasn't really undetectable, at least not yet. Having established that he had basic perceptibility, Allen now developed the physical characteristics of the most general sort, qualities that were shared by all manner of animate and inanimate objects.

When he became a young adult, he sometimes felt perfectly visible, as if there was no battle raging within his life between his beliefs and dreams and his actuality. He would spend hours in front of the dingy mirror in his room, flexing his muscles and smiling at the handsome young man who smiled back at him. He would study his face and physique carefully, believing he was, if not Paul Newman, at least not Lassie either. In fact, he had a featureless face, really, with just a few pimples and an unremarkable nose. His hair was a medium brown and his body was gangly. That is to say, he looked like every other kid in his school, except for the ones that were antagonized for being—in some small way—different.

There was always some child in the class who was preoccupied about proper name brands and places to purchase. One boy especially, Tony Carpenter, took delight in noticing the details of others' dressing habits and noting any improprieties. "Look at Russell. His pants didn't come from Boysen's Department Store. Boy, what a nerd. And look at Allen—fake Weejuns—man, what a geek. Hyuk. Hyuk." Allen, like every other teen at his school, could not have understood that by craving conformity, they sought the concealment of the pack. And being seen often meant being bullied.

Allen played baseball and had minor success at it. He was good enough to make the high school team and the American Legion team, but he didn't excel on either. He hit .257 and played back up right field. But when he did get to play ball, people saw him, and when he came up to bat, his father, if he could get away from work for the game, would call out from the bleachers, "Give it a ride, Allen." The coach knew who he was and when the lead was six or eight runs (for either team), he would look down the bench and send in Allen and three or four other fellows to field the last two innings. But Allen's baseball daydream remained, no, grew, for now the opening game no-hitter was followed by a perfect game, and after a couple more years of daydreaming, it became a game in which he struck out first fifteen, then twenty, make that twenty-seven batters. The game of baseball would never be the same.

And he still yearned for the attention of Karen Dobroski, who had become the most visible young lady in high school, with long blond hair that sported a new ribbon each day and a spring in her walk that could be described only as perky. Allen would make a point of walking down hallways where he knew Karen would be. For example, he might hang around the hallway where the business classes were taught because Karen had typing fourth hour. (Allen knew Karen's schedule as well as she did.) Sure enough, she would come bouncing down the hall, a gaggle of boys around her trying desperately to be seen. Allen always considered himself somehow above such a deliberate display of ogling and groveling, so kept his distance, leaning against the wall where the posters announced the DECA club bake sale later in the week. Karen giggled at the other boys' attention and looked right through Allen as she passed, seemingly deciding between a cupcake and a cookie when the sale came around. Sometimes, since Karen's focus was clearly somewhere twenty feet beyond where Allen stood, he had to turn around to see what she might have been looking at behind him. There was something about it that reminded him of when he was a child and his parents looked right through him to the playpen where Darlene bawled for some trivial need, even though Allen stood there with a perfect score on his math paper, complete with a gold star. It confirmed for Allen that while sometimes he could choose to be unseen, there were other times he could not help not being seen (especially by Karen). At those times he did not care for involuntary invisibility one bit. In a grander sense, however, Karen was a victim of her own visibility, and she never could have dreamed that she would be Allen's fantasy later that night while he was alone. Adults for some reason used to tell young men that masturbating would cause them to go blind, which oddly enough never deterred any young man from doing it. Alone in his room with his well-honed skill at reverie, Allen attempted to become blind in a manner as deliberate and unceasing as possible.

Once, in a brazen attempt at conspicuousness, Allen had actually gotten up the nerve to speak to Karen at school. She was at her locker in a rare moment of solitude, and Allen seized the moment.

"Hi, Karen."

She did not look around but managed a quiet, "Uh huh." Her hair was scented slightly, and Allen drank in the aroma. His head swam.

"You going to geometry now?" He blinked, watching her blonde hair flip back and forth from her locker to her book bag.

"Yeah, look, hold this for a minute, will you?" She turned around and, without looking at him, shoved in his arms a bedraggled stack of papers just as the bell rang for class. She slammed the locker shut, grabbed the papers out of Allen's arms, gave him a quick smile, and scurried off with a gentle, "Thanks, Alvin."

Allen's books fell to the floor in the transaction, a transaction that would have a completely different ending that night. Allen stood there for a moment, watched Karen flit around the corner, and then realized that he was late for history and that Karen had no clue who he was. He picked up his books and walked slowly to Mr. Whistle's history class.

It was some consolation to Allen that he could retreat to Mr. Whistle's classroom. Although Mr. Whistle looked like a bad Elvis impersonator wearing Liberace's clothes, Allen enjoyed the anti-establishment nature of the discussions in the class, which rarely had anything to do with history. Allen sat in the back of the history class, sulking and cursing terrible curses on his hiddenness, his own personal injustices, life, and everyone in general, except Karen, of course. She could not be blamed, since it wasn't her fault Allen was such an ordinary, awkward jerk, at least in his mind. That night, Karen was putty in Allen's sweaty, disgusting little hands as he suavely and passionately swept her off her feet and down the hall (past the DECA sign that was advertising yet another bake sale; these kids were evidently quite hungry) and into the teacher's lounge in which it was rumored that the teachers engaged in all manners of disgusting behavior of their own that should rightfully be reserved only for adolescents. When he opened his eyes, Allen vowed aloud, "Someday, Karen Dobroski, you will beg me to be your lover. Someday."

Though he did not like being invisible to Karen Dobroski, he continued sometimes to use his disappearing act to his advantage. In his senior English class, he discovered that he could disappear somewhere in the mass of adolescents and hide from his dreaded teacher, Mrs. Fitzmorris, who assigned essays that all seniors feared from the moment they entered high school. According to legend, Mrs. Fitzmorris had been left at the altar by a wealthy suitor through no fault of his own, but rather by that of the gravel truck that had popped him like an overfull balloon as he crossed the street on his way to the church. Her particular revenge on the world for the injustice of it all was to henceforth dress only in black, which punctuated her pallid, oversized face so that she looked like a Mrs. Potato Head (if you peeled the potato), and to force the seniors at Evanston High to write two-thousand-word essays, a practice that taught them more math than English. But somehow, despite her otherwise considerable skills in causing discomfort on each student who ever came before her, more often than not Mrs. Fitzmorris just could not find Allen. He never had to read his papers before the class. For some reason, his friend Joey almost always did, and his essays were verbatim from the *Encyclopedia Britannica*. Allen even managed to avoid writing one of the papers altogether. He was never even called to the board to diagram sentences, an exercise he was certain had no other point than to embarrass and torment high school seniors. (Should the line behind the verb slant when it was a transitive verb or a linking verb?)

Later that year, Allen graduated and marched across the stage in the gym. The graduates' parents endured the sweltering heat and the odor of dirty lockers that permeated the room, as much grateful and relieved as proud. Allen's parents cheered and clapped, and his two best pals, Joey and Carl, also attired in long black robes and flat cardboard hats, whistled and hooted. They had seen him. Most of the others in attendance—caught up in their own successes and all—had not, but it didn't matter. He was finished with high school, and now his life could begin. At least that's the way Allen saw it. All of his eighteen years had been in preparation for this great moment, the moment he would be freed from the grasp of his lost little hometown and his cruel high school teachers and his now elderly parents (his father, what, in his forties?) and be set loose upon the world at large. He epitomized all that was wonderful and promising in the Class of '76. He had elaborate day dreams about how his life would progress after high school, most of which were predicated on blazing success and perhaps a dose or two of fame, but, more importantly, some respect, or at least some acknowledgement.

Abstract Qualities

    Yet even that night Allen received further evidence of his occasional inconspicuousness and his lack of control over it. On the one hand, he felt so very special. He had, after all, just graduated from high school. Surely he glowed with an inner light that shone only in the graduated. Why, even Karen had said congratulations as they passed in the hallway of the school to see each other for the last time after twelve years of being invisible. At least he thought she was speaking to him; she seemed to be congratulating everyone. The image was one of a politician, shaking hands warmly, and telling her classmates, "Don't ever change. You'll go far. Don't ever change. You'll go far." It was what she had written in practically every yearbook in the school. Allen did not want to "not ever change," but he did hope to go far—far away from Evanston. For some reason, everything bad that happens to teenagers is the fault of the town in which they grew up. The good times are of their own doing. Yet nobody else took notice that night. When his parents took him to the Royal Royce for the twenty-piece fried shrimp dinner that night to celebrate, the waitress looked at Allen's father and mother as she took the orders for the rest of the family but only stared at her pad when Allen spoke. And when she brought out the orders, she placed the plates carefully in front of his parents and Darlene, but practically dropped the plate in front of Allen as if he were a phantom and the Johnsons had only ordered this plate to take home to the dog. When his glass of cherry flavored Sprite was empty, he tried to wave the waitress down, but she could never see him. Allen's father finally got her attention with one quick gesture. Allen was insignificant and obscure on this, the day of his crowning achievement. Had he truly spent his eighteen years in preparation for ever increasing and more oppressive invisibility? This he could not stand.

    Now Allen embarked on a more ambitious plan to combat his predicament. He would eschew the merely physical techniques in favor of the intellectual. Allen was too smart to remain unseen, at least in his scheme of things. He was ready to spring forth into the Real World. He believed his new plan for making a splash would set him on a path of excitement and glory.

Shape and Quantity

Every man takes the limits of his own field of vision for the limits of the world.
											-Arthur Schopenhauer

That summer after his high school graduation, Allen wrestled with a newfound level of frustration for his involuntary hiddenness and the new, grand scheme he would invoke to combat it. The episode in the restaurant had been his first adult experience with the phenomenon. Since it (like most phenomena of the universe) flew in the face of what he believed would occur (Allen had seriously thought that upon reaching adulthood, everything got easier, worries diminished, and in short, one ceased to be anonymous), it was all the more troubling to him. Allen Johnson had bona fide plans to prevent his becoming lost, and this summer would be the beginning of that wonderful arrangement. These plans were based upon his having a physicality that could not be denied. Allen Johnson was more than mere shape and color and mass; yes, he had arms and legs and a brain, but he also had dreams. Yes, Allen had dreams still, and they were as much a part of his nature as his fingers, although Allen didn't know it.

One of Allen's dreams as he entered this summer was that this would be the summer vacation to beat all summer vacations, the summer that all summers in history would henceforth be compared to ("Man, what a great summer. We toured the continent, we invented a cure for cancer, we even found another planet in the solar system. It was almost as good as Allen Johnson's summer after his senior year"). Yes, now Allen would be cast upon the world, more visible than ever, a force to be reckoned with, but when he sat down with his father the Sunday after graduation (Allen's dad evidently didn't want to spring things too quickly on the boy), the conversation was not what Allen had hoped it would be. They did not talk about Allen's idea of opening a baseball card shop in the little shopping center down the road while Allen lived at home with virtually no responsibilities except to eat and sleep (and listen to his stereo so loud that the walls shook, sometimes even when he had on earphones). No, they were not going to send him to Europe to ramble around and at some point, as if by magic, discover himself (Allen wasn't sure why one had to go someplace far away to discover one's self. Weren't you with yourself all along? But he was willing to give it a try). These had been more of Allen's carefully constructed daydreams that somehow, deep inside of Allen's head, he thought could actually come true.

But those dreams, like Allen, were vapors in a growing mist. Instead, his father had big news for Allen, all right, and he presented it with a grin of accomplishment. Mr. Johnson had secured a job for Allen with the Jimmy Jones Ford dealership for the summer. It seemed that Allen's father's cousin, Louis, was the used cars Assistant Sales Manager in training, and he had said he could use Allen's accumulated wisdom of twelve years of schooling to wash the used cars on the lot and, if the need arose, to occasionally hose down the lot itself.

Allen was devastated. This was supposed to be his summer, a summer of goofing off, hanging around with his friends, learning to drink beer and maybe, just maybe, getting an actual date with his neighbor and longtime fantasy, Karen Dobroski. (She had spoken to him at graduation, hadn't she? In fact, much of the grandness of Allen's dream summer was based upon securing the attention, then love, then virtue of Karen Dobroski, though just how one went about the last part was foreign to Allen.) The fact that he had spent every preceding summer goofing off and hanging around with his friends didn't matter. He had big plans for this summer. He was going to be seen. But his father spoke to Allen in a voice full of practicality and determination, and he pointed out to Allen that now that high school was finished, he needed to decide what he was going to do with his life. Now Allen knew why you had to go to Europe to find yourself. It wasn't that Europe was a better spot to discover the truths of one's inner self; it was because it was more fun than working at a car lot in the hot sun for two dollars and fifty cents an hour.

During this conversation, Allen was once again reminded that he was at times completely imperceptible, even to his own family. He started to explain to his father why he could not possibly take this fine position, though he was grateful for the opportunity, but his father went on talking, as if he could neither see nor hear Allen, about the many options to be found at the community college across town if Allen would just save up the money to pay half the tuition. Allen's father volunteered to pay the other half and to house and feed the young Johnson. The catch, of course, was that Allen must get and keep a job during the whole deal, an insidious plot to make permanent Allen's obscurity. Allen wanted to protest that this job was beneath him, that he was deserving of better things despite never before actually having had a job. But his father was going on now about the distant future (he was talking about what Allen might be doing some five years down the road!). Finally, resigned and defeated, Allen had gone up to his room, closed the door, and slipped into a deliberate and gloomy fog. He put on his earphones and played Jim Morrison so loud that anyone in the next room could have sung along with Jim as he tiptoed through "Killer on the Road" and went to sleep.

Allen awoke around eleven the next morning, still frustrated. His father left him directions to the Ford dealership, which everyone knew was on Frederickston Avenue, and instructions on how he should dress for this important meeting with his prospective employer, which was at one o'clock, exactly in the middle of the day so that Allen couldn't enjoy any part of the first day of the grandest summer vacation ever imagined. Allen dropped the note from his father and rolled his eyes. Why should he wear his sport coat, which was a size too small anyway, to talk to his dad's cousin about washing dirty Fairlanes?

Allen sat down to his breakfast of four bowls of Wheaties and spread the sports page in front of him. He tried to lose himself in the story about how the Reds were on a tear through the league, but Darlene came into the room. She in particular could see Allen all the time and took that ability as license to annoy him in any manner possible.

"Mom said you were a lazy bum for sleeping so late."

"Go away, Lotta." It was his secret weapon. She hated being called Little Lotta.

Darlene squinted her eyes. She braved for the fight. "Dad said you were going to have to start working every day and you'll have to get up early every day and that would be good for you. Maybe you might amount to something." She circled the table like a vulture.

"Drop dead, Lotta."

"Mom said you listened to too much rock and roll and that's what's wrong with you."

"Listen, Little Lotta, if you don't go away and leave me alone, I'm gonna knock you through a wall."

"Mom said I didn't need to be afraid of you and that if you knocked me through a wall, you'd have to clean up the mess." She still circled, just out of arm's reach.

"Okay, that's it." And he rose from the table to her shrieks as she darted from the room screaming, "Allen won't stop calling me Little Lotta!"

It was further evidence of the injustice of Allen's life. Not only was his summer about to be sabotaged, but his own parents were talking about him behind his back, trying to decide what was "wrong with him." There was nothing wrong with Allen except that he had an idiot sister and, like all other teenagers in the universe, parents who did not understand him. If everyone would just leave Allen alone, he would be fine. He tried to return to the story in the paper. Now where was he? Oh yes, Foster was hitting home runs.

"Allen, honey, shouldn't you be getting ready? Don't forget that you're supposed to be at Jimmy Jones Ford in an hour and a half." His mother floated into the room, her hair coiffed and an apron tied around her waist. June Cleaver would have been proud. She bustled about the kitchen, picking up Allen's bowl (although he was considering another bowl of cereal), and not focusing on Allen. While she glided through the room, she hummed a tune very quietly and smiled ever so slightly. Allen wondered why no one had told him about his mother's lobotomy. He thought about asking her about the discussion she and his father had evidently had about him while he was not around, but decided it was not worth it. What difference did it make? He knew they didn't understand him and that they still thought of him as a child even though he was eighteen years ripe and a high school graduate.

But Allen felt he was more important than that, more important than his parents gave him credit for. They just didn't have the tools to see him for who he really was. It was like those stupid jars and boxes downstairs that Allen's father kept, a veritable mountain of them now. Allen didn't need to collect jars and boxes. He was now too important, too visible to find any solace from mere order. In fact, Allen had decided his definition was informed at least in part by disorder. It was part of Allen's new plan to be visible. Allen had decided that his dad's ever-increasing assortment of canisters was an indication of some pathological need for order. He was convinced that it was evidence that his father, like the rest of his generation (how had they managed to survive?), had lost sight of the wonder and freedom that the unfettered world could provide. Real freedom was only possible if the nails, rubber bands, paper clips, and thumbtacks could all be thrown together in one glorious mess. If Allen ever needed a specific fastener, part of the expression of his freedom and his visibility was to dig through drawers and boxes until he happened onto something that might do.

It was an extension of Allen's definition, as he saw it. He was free to go through his life in a deliberate state of disorder and chaos. Certainly no one could ever force him to sort the nails from the screws. But his parents didn't know that. It was as if, as usual, they couldn't see who he really was. That was it. They couldn't see him despite his expressions of rebellion. He never made his bed and only cleaned his room when his father threatened him with physical harm. (Even then, he cleaned it very slowly.) They only needed a reminder. He needed to execute his plan in a new and daring way. He rose from the table and exited the room without speaking.

"There are clean towels in the closet, honey."

"Mmmph."

Allen showered, rolled on his Speed Stick, and admired his skinny but most certainly virile physique (if one looked with just the right squint), with white armpits in the mirror. He retreated to his room and sat on his bed for a moment, staring at the Rolling Stones poster on the wall that would have glowed fantastic colors under a black light (if Allen had a black light). Someday. Someday, he would have his own place, and he would have any kind of lights he wanted. He sat there and started to daydream about what his own place would look like. There would be parties and loud music; he would never have to pick up his clothes; he certainly would never make his bed.

"Allen, are you getting ready? You're supposed to be there in a little over an hour and it takes twenty minutes to get downtown." *How does she do that*, he wondered. How did she know he was not getting ready? But maybe he should be late (though Allen knew it didn't take anywhere near twenty minutes to drive anywhere in Evanston). Maybe if he was late, unfettered by the constraints of mere time, free and beyond the realm of societal norms, his distant cousin Louis would think he was irresponsible and wouldn't hire him. It was a way to put forth his plan. And surely then his parents would notice him if he screwed up the job deal. And then he could point out to his parents that it had been a lousy deal anyway and that there was no need for Allen to work. Allen had the rest of his life to work. If they would just leave him alone and let him play, they could see the real Allen Johnson shine forth.

"Allen, your good slacks are in the closet, and your white shirt is ironed and hanging right next to them." She wasn't going to make this easy.

"Okay, Mom. Uh, do you know where my tie is? I think I left it in Dad's Chrysler after graduation." It was a try.

"That's okay, honey. I'll go get one of your dad's ties for you to wear. Hurry now, or you'll be late."

That hadn't gone well, but Allen did not intend to give up so easily. He went ahead and dressed, trying hard to wrinkle the slacks and "accidently" dragging his shirt across the floor, but neither affected his appearance. He walked out of his room looking clean and presentable, although not exactly natty since his jacket sleeves were a good inch up his arms and his cowlick refused to lie down despite his heavy application of water. His mother caught him at the bottom of the steps and lassoed him with the tie that she had already knotted and loosened for him. She tightened it close around his neck, and Allen considered letting the lack of oxygen make him pass out or, better, kill him out right. But being averse to pain, he decided to loosen the tie with a grimace and a roll of the eyes that said, "Well, gee, why don't you just strangle me, Mom?" He stopped in the doorway and admired himself in the glass of the storm door.

Darlene was watching with a devilish look. "Have a nice day at the office, honey."

"Thank you, sweetheart. I'll see you later." He tried his best to give her a meaningful glare and evidently succeeded, judging from the immediate look of dread that crossed Darlene's face. "I think I lost the directions, Mom. Well, I'll try to find my way as best I can."

"Here they are." She smiled slightly and handed him the sheet of paper his father had written out. "Now, you know where Jimmy Jones Ford is. You go past it every time you go downtown. It's right there at the corner of Ninth and Frederickston." She was making this very difficult for him to miss.

"Well, I'd better go. I'll have to stop and get gas. I'm about out."

"Here, honey, take my car. You won't have time to stop along the way." She handed him her car keys, and he resigned and scuffled down the sidewalk. "Now don't dilly dally. You don't want to be late for your interview."

Yes, he did. But there's no chance for that with her shoving him out the door. He just couldn't believe his own mother couldn't see how miserable this was going to make him. She just couldn't see the real Allen Johnson, the Allen Johnson who was meant for bigger and better things than washing cars. Allen drove slowly all the way downtown, and he noticed that for the other drivers this day, not only was Allen invisible but evidently so was his mom's Buick Special. Cars pulled out in front of him at nearly every corner, and pedestrians walked out in the street, almost seemingly deliberate. It was more than Allen could stand.

"Jeez, watch where you're goin'," Allen yelled out the window at a white tuft of hair sitting in a dented Cadillac. "Hey! Christ! Where'd you get your license, Pete's Shoe Shop?" Allen waved his hand at a woman in a Pontiac who went on with her conversation with the man sitting next to her who was gripping the dash and staring ahead with his mouth agape. A small child on a bicycle rode toward the street, and Allen punched the brake. "Aiyeeee!"

By the time he arrived at the back entrance to Jimmy Jones Ford, Allen really was ten minutes late, but he was not happy about it. He was steaming mad.

He skulked through the garage doors where he had been told his second cousin would be waiting for him. He was met by a large, freckled, hump-backed man with a red crew cut, whose eyes folded slightly in the corner. Because his hair was closely cropped and because he was so heavy, Allen could not be sure if the man was twenty-five or forty-five. When he saw the man, Allen stopped and looked past to where a small office had been arranged in a corner of the garage. Beyond that, a door led to a tiny cubicle.

"What kin ah do fer you, young fella?" The man's voice was high-pitched and nasal and had an irritated sound about it.

"I'm looking for Louis Rowen. He's my cousin. I was supposed to meet him here at one," Allen said tersely. He had little patience for this lower-echelon type. (Who worked on used cars for Christ sake!)

"He don' work back here. He's over in the show room yonder." The redheaded behemoth pointed with his thumb to the glass facade across the parking lot. He turned, evidently considering the conversation finished.

"I'm pretty sure I was supposed to meet him out here. Could you call him?"

"Yeah, ah spect so." The large man sounded exasperated. "Hold on a sec." He stomped over to the desk, picked up the phone in one of his huge hands, punched a button and spoke gibberish for a moment. Then he nodded his head to the person on the other end of the line as if the other person could see him. The manner in which he walked and held the phone made Allen think that he probably was a powerful, though odd-looking, man.

"Well, he ain't back yet from lunch, but ah spect he'll be along 'bout any time. Come on in an' set, if you wanna. Ah told 'em you's out here." Allen walked past the man and sat on one of the army surplus chairs in front of the army surplus desk in the corner. The man sat in the other chair and watched Allen out of the corner of his eye. Allen decided that anyone so large, so strange looking, and so relaxed in a garage must have some sort of disability. The huge man eyed Allen slowly and deliberately. *Well, at least this moron can see me*, Allen thought. The two of them sat there in the quiet, and Allen began to notice how warm this June afternoon was becoming. The air was heavy with motor oil, and he heard the slow droning of a gargantuan fly buzzing futilely against the grimy window, trying as hard as Allen to escape from the garage. The other fellow sat there studying Allen as if he didn't know what to make of him. They sat for several minutes, which seemed much longer to Allen, and neither spoke.

Finally, Allen saw the familiar face of his cousin, Louis, coming through the garage doors. Louis strutted across the garage, the flared legs of his charcoal gray leisure suit flapping against each other. Allen rose to meet him, but the redheaded fellow only grunted, turned around in his chair, and began shuffling some papers on the desk.

"Hi, Allen. Sorry I'm late. Tell you the truth, I clean forgot we were supposed to meet today." So much for Allen's plan. "Well, I see the two of you have already met." Louis was pumping Allen's hand as if Allen had just bought a new truck. Allen couldn't help but notice that Louis's hand had a moist, puffy feel to it.

"Jimbo, this here is Allen. Mr. Jones said for you to take him and work him on the used cars." Jimbo turned, eyed Allen suspiciously, and extended his hand. Allen reached out his hand, and Jimbo took hold of it in a vice grip. Allen felt simultaneously a sharp popping pain in his palm and a tear springing up in his eye. Jimbo dropped his hand, and Allen flexed the now bonded bones. Jimbo shook his head as if Allen had failed some test.

"What do ah need him fer? Ah don' need no hep out chere. Dere somphin wrong wid what ah'm doin'?"

"No, no, Jimbo. This here's my cousin. He's just gonna help out this summer. You can use some help, can't you?" Allen was speechless. Not only did the moron Jimbo not want him, but the moron Jimbo would be his boss.

"What's he gonna do? He ever do any engine work?" They were speaking about him as if he were not standing there between them. "Ah don' need no jackleg out here what ah gotta keep an eye on."

"No, no, it won't be like that. Old Allen here, he'll work real hard, won't you Allen?" He didn't wait for Allen to respond. Allen wanted to say, "Hell no, I'm not going to do anything for this pea-brained halfwit," but he wasn't even looked at. "Allen's not a mechanic, but he can wash cars and run errands for you. You give him a job, and Allen will do it." He slapped Allen on the back approvingly. "Besides, Mr. Jones already approved it." And with that, Louis spun around and walked out of the garage. Jimbo looked hard at Allen, then shrugged and turned back around in his chair.

"Dere's a Mustang out back needs warshin'. Stuff's agin da back wall. Get it done aforn two." Allen looked at his watch, but before the time could register in his brain, he realized that he was wearing his good clothes.

"Well, I gotta . . ."

"You can't do it, dat's fine. Go on home, boy." Jimbo didn't turn around or even raise his head from his papers. Now Allen was torn. He could go home, say he didn't get the job, and have his summer back, or he could just go back there and show this lummox how a clean Mustang should look. Besides, Louis would probably talk to Allen's father about it, and then there would be a stink. No, he might just as well wash the damned Mustang and start working on the destruction of his summer. He walked slowly and dejectedly to the back and found the cleaning supplies, took off his jacket and tie, and started washing the mud-caked car he found behind the garage.

When Jimbo came shuffling around the corner at two, the car sat gleaming, and Allen was a sweating, filthy mess. His white shirt was streaked with grime from the tires, and his good blue slacks were three different shades of black. "You done? Gwan over an' git dem tars an' wag 'em in here so's we kin change de tars on dis Galaxy. Yor cousin say he needs it on de lot by t'morry." Allen dropped his shoulders. Nothing like the "Give it a ride, Son!" his father used to say. He tossed the hose to the side and went over to the stack of tires Jimbo had waved at and started lifting off the first tire. "When you git done wid dat, come git dis drum of trash an' take it yonder an' burn it." Jimbo went back into the garage, and Allen rolled the first tire in through the door.

It went like that for the rest of the day. No sooner did Allen finish one job than Jimbo would have two more for him. By the time four-thirty came and Jimbo started closing up the garage, Allen was exhausted and defeated. His only satisfaction was that the garage closed earlier than he thought. Allen picked up his coat and his father's tie in his grimy hands (putting permanent grease stains on both) and walked out to his mother's car.

Jimbo stood next to the garage and called after Allen. "Be here at seven-thirty t'morry. And don' wear no sissy clothes. T'morry ah got some hard stuff fer ya." Allen thought there was a certain malice in his tone.

Great, he thought. Today wasn't hard, but tomorrow will be. "Ah'll tell you what, boy, you done okay t'day, considerin'. You jes remember, they's ain't nothin wrong wid a man what some hard work won't fix it. But you gonna hafta take mo' pride in yo' job, son. You work hard an' bulieve in yo'self, an' you'll do awright. Whut a man does is whut a man is, an' don' ferget it."

Great, that's what I need, Allen thought, *the Gospel according to The Thing*. None of this was going according to plan. Allen was not becoming more important; if anything, he was vanishing more quickly, and his scheme of visibility through chaos was failing miserably. Allen drove home in a funk of misery and defeat.

Measure

A youth with his first cigar makes himself sick; a youth with his first girl makes other people sick.

-Mary Wilson Little

Jimbo had not lied; the next day was harder than the previous, and the next even harder, and so on. By the time the next Saturday came, Allen was so sore and tired that he could barely get out of bed. Allen became painfully aware of the limits of his body, the extent of its mettle. But he would soon discover other measures in his life that weren't painful to learn. It was the uncovering of these facts of Allen's being that made the realization of his dialectic so agonizing. Having become defined in a physical sense, Allen Johnson was destined to discover the essential difference of his inner self from his physical self. But that comes later. For now, Allen needed to find the measure of his external self.

Each day at the garage, every time Allen finished a task, Jimbo would give him another, less pleasant task. That summer, salesmen came and went, and they never knew Allen's name. Except for his signature on Allen's paltry pay check, the owner never took any notice of Allen's work at the lot.

That was how Allen first got started on a new and more frustrating form of obscurity: the unseen worker. He arrived every morning before most folks were out and about and performed slave labor for so little pay that no one, not even the boss, would even notice. When Mr. Dobroski came in later that summer to buy the Mustang so Karen could take it to college, nobody knew that it was Allen who had made it shine (except Allen, who took a meager pleasure from the knowledge and somehow turned it into a perverse fantasy that night). Allen felt that his talents and time were being wasted, and he daydreamed that he would run off to some far away, glittering city to start his life anew, where people would see and appreciate him. Things would be fine if he just took off to St. Louis and became a disc jockey or something glamorous like that. But no, he would have to stay in this little dead end job, not at all certain what he might do with his life, taking orders and occasional lectures from Jimbo, the Socratic Chief Mechanic and Sumo Wrestler. Allen felt utterly lost.

The only time anyone did notice Allen at the car dealership was that one hot July day when he had been standing in the lot next to the car dealership burning trash and a car full of girls who graduated with Allen drove by and hooted and called to Allen. *That's fine*, he thought. The one time he wished no one would see him, a whole car load of girls had seen him.

What he didn't realize was that a young lady named Beth Ann Hollis was in the car. While she had hooted at Allen with the other girls, she also noticed that a month of slave labor dished out by Jimbo The Thing had turned Allen into a stout looking young man, and she was more than a little impressed. After that sighting, she tried to get Allen to notice her by finding reasons to drive down by the car lot during the day, or perhaps even driving in his neighborhood in the evenings on the chance he was out cruising with his buddies. She was having no success until she saw him sitting in the Dairy Drive-In one Saturday eating French fries while Joey sat next to him and rambled on about the future of automotive exhaust design. Beth Ann parked her car and walked nonchalantly next to Allen's, sensuously sipping her vanilla phosphate and pretending not to notice him. She leaned on his bumper and carried on a halfhearted conversation with her best friend Vicki, who had also walked nonchalantly next to Allen's Pinto, until he finally looked up and his eyes focused and he suddenly realized there was a girl on his bumper. Joey was in the middle of a lengthy explanation of how they could both be rich if they could only invent a device for cleaning the insides of exhaust pipes when he realized that Allen was staring with his mouth open at something in front of the car. But when Joey looked, all he saw was Beth Ann Hollis from his Civics class.

"What's wrong, Allen?"
"Who's that?"
"Who?"
"Her."
"You mean her?"
"Yeah, her," Allen said, exasperated. "Who is she?"
"That's just Beth Ann. You know, Bobby Hollis's little sister."
"Uh huh." But Allen was already gone. He fairly jumped out of the car but then slowed his gait and sauntered up to Beth Ann. "Hi. My name's Allen." He was trying to sound suave, but it seemed to Allen he sounded

like a little kid, so he lowered his voice an octave before saying, "You're Beth Ann, right?"

"Uh huh." She tried not to start at the shift in his voice, and then she slowly walked towards her own car. It was a tried and true device for Beth Ann. By making herself very obvious to a boy then pretending she did not notice him, she could make him try fifteen different ways to make her notice him. He would fret and scheme for her attention until he was exhausted, and then she would reel him in. Allen did not disappoint her.

Allen called Beth Ann nightly for a week and finally persuaded her to go to a movie (in the meanwhile, Beth Ann and Vicki had checked out all the movies to be sure Allen picked just the right movie to invite Beth Ann to: *Ode to Billy Joe*) and then they went to a party at Vicki's house (Allen believed it was only a fortunate coincidence that Vicki decided to have a party). Having gone to a party together, according to the rules of adolescent dating, they were officially transformed into a couple. Although Allen had dated some girls before, he was captivated by Beth Ann (who maintained a balance between coy and cloy that kept Allen completely off balance), and for some reason he decided that maybe he should start thinking about his future (dishevelment having failed as well as being unwelcome by Beth Ann, whose opinions suddenly impinged on a great deal of Allen's thought processes).

After talking it over with Joey and Carl, Allen decided that he needed a new plan to overcome his lack of visibility, so he resolved to attend the community college. Allen informed his father that his friends and he had decided that they should consider the future and that perhaps college was an option, and the elder Mr. Johnson had only sighed and shook his head. Before Allen even realized it, he had mapped out his own future for the next five years.

The rest of the summer took on a different light for Allen. Instead of a summer destroyed, he now looked at his days with a new appreciation. He worked harder than ever at the car lot, although Jimbo didn't seem to notice. He only gave Allen more work to do. Allen realized that, in fact, Jimbo was incapable of very much sympathy and probably resented having another person around, but Allen practiced his disappearing act and made himself scarce around the redheaded Sumo Wrestler. He even found a certain pleasure in the passing of the days until night would come and he could drive by Beth Ann's house. And Allen found that even during the most unpleasant tasks, since all the tasks were utterly menial, he could escape into a reverie. At the same time that he washed a car, he could be valedictorian of his class at college, eagerly sought by business leaders and the government alike.

Meanwhile, after work, Allen and Beth Ann became inseparable; Joey and Carl rarely saw Allen unless it was a Sunday morning and Beth Ann was at church. Otherwise, Allen basked in the attention he received from Beth Ann (as well as the singularity of focus his attempts at blindness now took on). Then, later that summer, the attention he was receiving took on an entirely different light. In the first place, Allen felt that Beth Ann saw him completely, and the importance that gave him made him want to see her—all of her. While she put him off for a while, eventually they discovered the facts of their own and each other's existence in detail.

The primary fact that Allen discovered was that one cannot avoid one's own sexuality. It was fated, perhaps, that he discovered this while sitting at The Strand Movie House watching The Omen with Beth Ann clutching his arm close to her breast lest the demon attack her (Allen placed a large empty popcorn box on his lap in response). Although she pretended to be offended, she couldn't help her feeling of appreciation for either his decency at being embarrassed or his indecency at being so aroused by her. At any rate, she expressed very eloquently her appreciation later that night while they sat in Allen's '74 Pinto in her driveway.

Allen went home in a fog of satisfaction and infatuation.

After that, Allen and Beth Ann vanished. Joey and Carl did not see Allen for weeks on end (a fact that, on the one hand, put them off a bit, and, on the other hand, made them quite jealous). Even Allen's family began to notice that they didn't see Allen around the house. When Beth Ann and Allen went to the Jerry's Drive-In and Coffee Shop, they sat in a corner, huddled up, staring goo-goo-eyed at each other. The waitresses didn't bother to wait on them most often, or if they did, it was only to bring them a soda and the ticket. Allen even started attending Beth Ann's church sometimes, sitting inconspicuously in the back of the congregation with her. One Sunday, the preacher, who was more cerebral than officious, took as his lesson for the flock the evils of sins of the flesh, and Allen had squirmed and fidgeted throughout the sermon, wondering how the preacher knew or who had told on them. Beth Ann, on the other hand, sat as still as stone. When Allen reached for her hand, she had pulled away and placed her hands folded in her lap.

"When the body is sullied," Reverend Pondermust explained, "the mind is also sullied." Allen had to agree with that, given the nature of his thoughts every waking moment and many of the sleeping ones too. "One must, if he will purify his thoughts, forego the distractions of the physical. The mind and the body are inseparable in this respect." The good preacher waved his arms towards his congregation and looked out over his glasses which had slid down his nose. Now he removed his glasses and pointed with the earpiece. "But there is an important difference between the body and the spirit, for while the body may find no pleasure in the lack of gratification, the mind will find fulfillment in the resulting purification of thought." Allen considered that for a while and decided that there may be a certain truth to the preacher's point, but Allen and Beth Ann forgot the lesson that afternoon on a lonely stretch of country road that seemed to dead end into a stand of mottled trees.

The next Sunday, Reverend Pondermust spoke of the sins of lust. Allen had squirmed, and Beth Ann had pulled away, and both of them avoided the knowing look that the preacher seemed to be throwing their way. Actually, that look was a skill the shepherd had learned from his mentor. "Everyone is guilty of sin, my son. If you look at them like you know what their particular sin is, they will quake under your gaze and throw more money in the plate in order to absolve themselves." Allen didn't throw more money in and guiltily shook the preacher's dry, limp hand as he passed through the doors after the sermon. He and Beth Ann tried to keep their thoughts pure for the rest of the day, but when they were alone on a narrow stretch of gravel alongside the river, lust overtook them and they wrestled frenetically there on the riverbank. When their passions were sated, they rolled apart, and a group of four old men in Red Man caps started applauding from the top of the bank where they had sat down to watch. Beth Ann cried and scrambled to straighten herself, and Allen had hustled her to his car. They drove off in a cloud of gravel, dust, and catcalls.

The more Beth Ann and Allen saw of each other, the less other people saw of them. But, of course, this was a different sort of vanishing for Allen. This was, in a sense, a deliberate disappearing, much like stealing the candy that time at the five and dime had been, and Allen was completely satisfied with his transparency.

Then, when August started waning, the inevitable occurred and Allen-and-Beth-Ann became Allen and Beth Ann again, since she was already scheduled to attend school over in Bowling Green and Allen was still planning to stay home to attend college. (He hadn't actually applied yet, but there was plenty of time for that: school didn't start for another week and a half.) So on a hot Saturday afternoon, Allen and Beth Ann said a tearful good bye to each other that resulted in a furious burst of passion in the rear seat of Allen's Pinto. He took her home and drove to his own home with a mixed feeling of regret and physical satisfaction.

He sat in his room and tried to figure out how sad or happy he was and felt a very odd feeling come over him. Suddenly, he wondered how Beth Ann felt. He tried to return to the physical gratification that he had felt, but his mind kept returning to Beth Ann and how she looked with her eyes moist and slightly reddened with sorrow. Now this was most troubling for Allen. He paced about in his room, looked up at his Rolling Stones poster, and decided he didn't really love that poster all that much after all. He stepped across the little piles of dirty clothes on the floor and sat heavily on the edge of his bed. He looked across the room to his record collection, but there was nothing to which he wanted to listen. He kept seeing Beth Ann, and he wondered if she was seeing him.

She was.

Quality

O physics! Preserve me from metaphysics!

-Isaac Newton

Allen Johnson survived his first summer of adult life (at least as he saw it). And if his plot to achieve visibility, or at least notoriety, through a deliberate exercise in disorder and dishevelment had failed, he could not complain too bitterly about the pains of his indiscernibility that summer. But now he embarked on a more telling span of invisibility—the oblivion of the random undergraduate college student. To be sure, at least part of that transparency resulted from the reflection on his life that college afforded Allen. As he wound his way through the curriculum, his instructors enticed him to use his own experiences, meager though they may have been, as examples at every turn. The outcome of all this thinking about his life was that Allen's being, his very existence, was counterbalanced by what he was not being, which was ever present to him. He was the central point in an unending struggle between his existence and his nothingness, between what he was becoming and what he could not be. When Allen recognized fleeting images of himself, it was because he could also recognize the phantasm that was not him. Realizing what he was not provided for a deepening battle in Allen.

    He did not realize all of this would occur when he drove over to the community college to apply, register, and enroll the day before classes began. He found that the entrance to the community college was indistinguishable from the entrance to the Mr. Wiggs department store next door. Somehow, Allen found the right building and eventually the right door and went directly to the end of the longest line he had ever seen. The line stretched down the long corridor and around the corner out of sight. He stood at the end of the line, his application from the back page of the local paper wadded up in his hands. (On the other side was a large picture of the new Cob Queen with a description of her likes, "disco music and men who speak Italian," and dislikes, "Heavy metal and street people." Also on the other side, squeezed in next to the picture of the Cob Queen, was a brief article on the upcoming presidential election.) Then Allen realized he might not be in the right line to register for classes, so he decided to ask the girl in front of him, although she might have been just as lost as he was.

"Is this the line to register for classes?"

"Yes, it is." She barely turned her head sideways to respond.

"Thanks." Allen watched her return her gaze forward. She was familiar, somehow. "Excuse me, don't I know you? Did you go to Evanston Senior last year?"

"No, I'm a sophomore." She wagged her pony tail with an air of superiority and again did not turn completely around so Allen felt almost humiliated for having asked. He also saw that his pride at being a high school graduate was ill founded. You were nothing until you were a sophomore at the community college, evidently.

Allen waited in line, shuffling forward two or three steps at a time, for two hours. When he arrived at the doorway of the room that he thought was where the line ended, he saw that the room was huge and full of tables where the line broke into dozens of individual lines. A tired man in a faded tweed jacket stood in the doorway, looked at Allen's application and directed him to a table where another tired looking man in a faded herringbone jacket took his application and spoke to him in a monotone without looking up.

"Major?"

"Uh, I'm not sure."

"Undecided. Table C." He waved Allen over to a table where some twenty other young people were already standing.

"No, I mean philosophy. I want to major in philosophy." Allen wasn't really sure what philosophy was, but he knew they taught it in college. Now the man looked up at Allen, peering slowly over his bent half glasses that perched at an angle on the tip of his very long nose.

"Philosophy?"

"Yeah, I want to be a philosophizer." Now the man grinned, took off his glasses and pointed with them to a lonely table at the far end of the room where another tired looking man in a faded corduroy jacket sat, but no students were waiting.

"Go on over, and talk to Dr. Kamew."

Allen went over and talked with Dr. Kamew, and the entire time they talked, Allen tried to see if there was something lodged in Dr. Kamew's throat that made him talk with a funny airy sound that made it seem as if he were perpetually sighing as he spoke.

"Yesss, can I hellp youh?" No, there wasn't anything in Dr. Kamew's mouth.

"Uh, yes sir. That man over there said I should talk with you. I want to go to college." This evidently amused Dr. Kamew because he leaned back and smirked.

"Ohh, youh dooh, dooh youh?" He took the new piece of paper that the man at the table had handed Allen.

Was that cotton in his cheeks? No, Allen couldn't see any. "Yeah, I mean, yes sir."

"Hand hwhat exactly whould youh like tooh dooh in collehge, Mhister Jhohnsohn, is it?"

No, no foreign objects were protruding from his neck. "Well, I was considering maybe philosophy." Allen wasn't sure why he was keeping this up, exactly. He had only said philosophy because he hadn't wanted to stand in line at the other table, but this didn't seem like the spot to come clean. If he could just get his schedule and get out of here, he would go home and hide for the rest of the day rereading the letter he received from Beth Ann earlier this week.

"Philosophy. Whell, whell. Let's seeh what whe can dooh. Why don't whe just put youh in mhy hethics clahss stahting tomorrowh mornhing." And as the man scribbled on the paper, Allen also realized that, yes, this was Dr. Kamew's everyday speech and that, yes, Allen would be listening to this for at least an entire semester. "Hand whyh don't whe put youh in English one hoh one, hand perhahps bhiology . . ."

But Allen had stopped listening. Instead, Allen daydreamed about his letter from Beth Ann. She had written that she was thinking about him, but she had also written about some sort of freshman mixer and something about rush and about her roommate and about her schedule. There felt like maybe something more was being left out, but Allen couldn't figure out what that might be. Now Dr. Kamew was handing the piece of paper to Allen, so he returned his attention to the professor.

"Soh, Ih ghuess whe'll seeh youh tomorrowh morhning, Mihsterh Jhohnson." And with that, Dr. Kamew extended his hand. Allen remembered the pain he had felt from Jimbo's death grip and that the only defense for a hard handshake was to grip tightly first. Besides, Jimbo had explained to Allen how a first handshake is a kind of test of a man's character, and Allen didn't want to fail his first test in college. Allen didn't think about how much two and half months of manual labor had strengthened him. He took Dr. Kamew's hand and squeezed as hard as he could. Dr. Kamew's puffy hand gave under his grip, and Allen saw the pain shoot up the professor's arm and bulge his eyes out and come down the other arm so that his corduroy jacket shook. Allen let go of the mushy hand, and the professor's eyes narrowed. "Yes, we will see you tomorrow, Johnson," Dr. Kamew said now in a lower voice as he rubbed his hand.

Allen figured Dr. Kamew would have it out for him, all right, and he wanted to explain that it was all a mistake, but it seemed pointless to carry on about it. So he walked away determined to disappear in that ethics class.

Allen waited in some more lines and finally left the building a college student, and something about that sounded good to Allen. He was a college student. All he needed was a coffee shop to sit in now, although he didn't really care for coffee too much. He might want to grow his hair longer, too, he decided. He drove home and retrieved his letter from its hiding place under his mattress, and read it again.

Allen felt an odd melancholy come over him as he realized what it was that was being said in the letter without being said: Beth Ann was embarking on a path that would include Allen less and less as the weeks went by. While perhaps this should have upset Allen more than it did, he couldn't help but be happy for the gleeful, exuberant tone in Beth Ann's letter.

Allen went out driving, his Jim Croce tape blaring from the eight-track. He drove by Joey's house, but he was at his job over at Mario's Pizza Emporium, and Carl had already gone off to Vincennes to start school there, so Allen was left to his own devices. He drove far out into the flat countryside down roads he and Beth Ann had explored on lazy Saturday afternoons. Before too long, Allen was out of town and alone on a deserted strip of grey-black pavement that stretched on before him until it melted into the sky with heat waves. Finally, Allen stopped the car in the middle of the road and stared at the rows and rows of tall corn, now yellowing. On the stump of a dead red oak, a meadowlark sang a twill before it flew off. Filled with a kind of good, melancholy feeling, Allen's mind wandered to the ironies of change and the passing of people through our lives, and he sighed and spoke out loud to himself.

"So this is what life . . ."

"Hey, Stupid!" Allen jumped in his seat. "What the hell do you think you're doin'?" Allen had not seen the pickup truck pull up behind him.

"Excuse me, is this your private road? Jeez!" And the truck pulled around him, and the driver, an old man wearing a John Deere cap, glared at Allen as he fumbled with the gears on the Pinto.

Allen felt a dark cloud in his head. Again, he had what started out as a relatively good day turn suddenly into a very frustrating one. It just didn't seem fair somehow. *Why does something always happen to mess up my life*, he thought. He decided that, as bad as it was to be at home where no one understood him, it was probably better than this. He drove off down the lane. He turned at the next road so he could return to town, but the farther he drove, the less familiar the road seemed, and finally, as the sun began to turn orange, Allen realized he was hopelessly lost. The dark cloud in Allen's head grew darker. At long last he spotted a building, for there was little along the road except field after field of corn with an occasional field full of cattle thrown in for variety. When he neared the building he saw that it was an old general store with two tired gas pumps outside and a hand lettered sign on the side that read "Okra Cash and Carry."

Allen stopped the car in front of a pump (he suddenly realized he was nearly out of gas) and trudged up the wooden plank steps that led to the porch of the store. Inside, the homemade shelves painted white held a paltry selection of canned goods and hardware. The screened door with the Colonial Bread sign slammed behind Allen as he entered, and a haggard woman with a face like a five-pound bag of Idahos glanced at him before going on with the conversation she was having with a wiry little man who must have been seventy-five. His face was deeply creased by overexposure to the sun and years of squinting.

"Well, I'll tell you what," the old man was saying, "I don't know what's to happen when you cain't git the old cow to give no more milk. It's a damn shame. She won't produce, and now what do I do? I'll tell you what, I don't like it when I'm faced with it, no ma'am." Allen waited with growing impatience.

"Yep, I know what you mean, Mr. Waller. Me, I gotta old hen what don't lay no more, and she ain't no good for cooking, so I guess I gotta feed her or kill her. I hate to think about it. Why that old hen's been with me for years. She's like one of the family." The woman was rocking slowly in her chair, though it wasn't a rocker. Allen stood expectantly for the conversation to be over.

"Oh yeah, well, I'll tell you what, a hen don't eat all that much. You keep that old girl around. Lord, I hope they feed me when I get too old to work." The old man leaned familiarly on the counter.

"I don't imagine that'll happen, Mr. Waller. You'll be pushin' that plow long after I'm pushin' daisies, I'd say." Allen stood incredulous. The entire conversation seemed both totally mindless and endless. What's more, it went on unabated even though he was standing there right next to them, as if—well, of course Allen knew—he was invisible.

"Excuse me," Allen finally broke in. The old man turned and gave him a searing look of contempt for his lack of respect, but the woman only sat up in her chair behind the counter that ran along the side of the store.

"Hep ya?"

Allen looked gratefully at the woman. "Yeah, I mean, yes ma'am. I need some gas and directions on how to get back to Evanston."

"Lost, huh?" Her voice was gravely but soft, and she had a friendly, satisfied look about her. "Well, you ain't the first, and I dare say you ain't the last. Folks alla time driving out and get turned around. I guess one country road looks like another to the untrained eye." She winked a friendly wink at Allen, and he felt a relief. At least he would get home sometime tonight. The woman sent Allen out to pump three dollars and forty cents worth of gas (that was what he could scrounge up) and when he came back up the steps, he noticed how the growing darkness made the yellow, golden light from inside seem even more inviting. When Allen came back in, the woman was standing to the side of the counter drawing a map on the back of a brown paper bag. She wasn't even five feet tall but had a solid look to her, and Allen felt very reassured.

"Okay, look here," she sidled alongside Allen. "You go on down here to the big white church an' turn right," she waved with her right hand. "Now it don't look like much of a road, but it'll get you there. Stay on that until you come to a sycamore grove."

"A sycamore grove?"

"Yeah, a sycamore grove. You can't miss it. Big trees with whitish trunks. You'll see 'em. Now just beyond that on the left, you'll see a little road about fifty yards up. It'll look like maybe a driveway or somethin' but it goes through." Allen's confidence was fading. "That road will dead end into the River Road. Now be careful you don't miss the turn. It ain't marked with a stop sign or anythin', but if you go too far, you'll get wet." She winked at Allen with that same familiar wink. Allen just stood there nodding. "Go right on the River Road, and then you stay on that till you come to a tee. Turn left an' you're inta Evanston." Allen stood there, filled with doubt. "Or you could go the way you come, but it's a lot farther t'go that way."

"Thanks, thanks a lot," Allen muttered as he walked to the door studying the map that he realized would be impossible to see in the darkness outside.

"Whatsa matter, son? You 'fraid you won't get back? Don't worry, boy. You gotta have some faith, son. Ya know, faith is what will sustain you when all else fails. There ain't a lot you can control in life, but you kin choose to believe. Doncha' see, son, once you see you gotta choice, it's just a matter of choosing. That ain't hard. Now you can go back that other way if'n ya wanna, but now that you know there's a better way, why would you? All you gotta do is make up your mind that you gonna go the new way, and you got it." She winked at Allen when he looked up at her. Allen hoped she was better at giving directions than she was at preaching.

With the help of the full moon that had risen just after dark, Allen found his bearings and way back okay. After a little bit, the roads became familiar, and then suddenly he was into Evanston driving down Frederickston not a half mile from the Ford dealership. Allen passed the garage where he would be tomorrow after class and thought it looked even uglier by night. There was nothing in the least to romanticize about his job. It appeared that a light was on in one corner of the garage, but Allen was not interested in stopping to check it out.

When Allen finally arrived in front of his house, he felt a heavy dose of relief come over him. The house was lit up with a light on in every room (as usual). Allen wasn't expecting a party, or even to find his parents worried, but when he came into the house and saw that no one had even noticed he was at least four hours late, he was disappointed. Upstairs from his sister's room, he could hear Barry Manilow claiming to write the songs. In the den, his father was snoring over the subdued sounds of Monday night baseball droning on the television. Allen went into the kitchen to find his mother had left a plate of, by now, very dry, very tough pork chops with apple sauce and green beans all bleeding together in the oven and a note explaining that tonight was Bunko night. Instead, Allen ate four bowls of Wheaties and went to bed.

The next day Allen started college, and with one notable exception his first day of college was less stressful than his last day of summer had been. He eventually found his classes, although he wondered what sort of illogic was used to number the rooms. He even saw some of his former schoolmates in some of his classes, but no one that he knew well. All his friends had applied elsewhere except Joey, who had forgotten to apply anywhere. In the end, Allen decided things were going pretty well. Most of his classes dismissed early since it was the first day and none of the students had thought to buy books yet. In each class, Allen had found a spot to sit somewhere in the middle and towards the back of the classroom. It would be his seat for the rest of the semester, since once a student stakes out a seat, it is a major breach of protocol for another student to take that seat in any subsequent meeting of that class. If he wanted, Allen could melt into the mass of young adults and disappear much as he had in high school. But Allen had endured enough invisibility and he was determined not to disappear. In each class, he raised his hand and asked the teacher a question regarding the grading or perhaps the length of papers that were required. The other students took no notice of Allen, but the instructors called on him and looked deliberately at his face. All in all, Allen felt quite visible, thank you very much.

Everything was going along smoothly until Allen went to his ethics class where Dr. Kamew was waiting. As soon as Allen entered the classroom, he knew he was in trouble. Dr. Kamew saw him walk in and started rubbing his hand that had been crushed, although as Allen saw it, he had not really squeezed all that hard. But the professor looked hard at Allen and watched him go to his seat in the same general spot he had sat in other classes. Allen would not be able to vanish in this class even if he wanted to. Dr. Kamew stopped glaring at Allen and went back to fiddling with some cards on the dais behind which he was standing. Allen felt a great weight of dread on his back as he sat, and, out of fatigue, he plopped his notebook down on the desk. It struck the hollow surface sounding like the report of a gun and echoing down the hallways. Dr. Kamew jumped as if he had been jabbed by an electric prod, his note cards that he had been sorting and resorting flew into the air and fluttered down like giant faded snowflakes.

"Jeezus Chrise!" Dr. Kamew was standing there shaking. The other students snickered then laughed at the comedy of his overreaction, except of course for poor Allen who sat there with his head in his hands staring blankly.

"Uh, sorry."

"Yes, Mister Johhnsohn, so I seeh." Dr. Kamew tried his best to regain his composure, but it was too late. The entire class had eventually broken into a raucous laughter when he let go of the cards, and the more the students thought about it, the more they laughed. Any control over how he would be perceived by the students had been lost. Allen had tried not to laugh, but because laughter is by nature contagious, the more the other students laughed and snickered, the more Allen wanted to until he was also giggling over the sight of those carefully arranged, yellowing note cards (how many years had Dr. Kamew used them?) floating unceremoniously to the ground. Dr. Kamew glowered at Allen, and he just sat there giggling. While Dr. Kamew plotted his revenge, Allen plotted his disappearance.

Substance and Accident

A woman never forgets her sex. She would rather talk with a man than an angel any day.
                                                    -Oliver Wendell Holmes

Allen tried several tactics to succeed in that ethics class, as well as in his other courses and his job. One result from these various attempts was that Allen began to recognize, subtly, that these compiled different experiences had provided him with understanding of the basis of his own permanence. As his experiences were reinforced, he began to see that the things that occurred in his life were not isolated but were within a stream of occurrences. And when the same things happened over and over again, it was because something (it might even be Allen himself) was the same. And if experiences would be altered, there must be a cause to that change.

In his college life, this meant discovering the causes of his understandings and what might cause change in them. In his ethics class, he at first tried to disappear somewhere in the back, but Dr. Kamew made a point of calling on poor Allen whenever a tough question came up. When this first happened, Allen was not ready for the question and sat there silently, not knowing the answer or how to gracefully get out from under the question.

"Whell, Mihsterh Jhohnsoh, how would youh characterhize Bhentham's cahlculhus of hethical behavhior?" Dr. Kamew had asked. And poor Allen had sat there, embarrassed and silent although he had read the assigned chapter. He just didn't quite get the content clearly. Dr. Kamew stood smugly victorious before the class waiting in silence for what seemed like hours while Allen squirmed.

Finally, Allen said meekly, "I don't understand the concept of . . ."

Old Dr. Kamew was armed and ready, "Whell, pherhahps hif youh had rhead the hassignmhet, Mhisterh Jhohnsohn." And then he went on to explain the theory until it was as clear as a bowl of mud to every student in the class. In general, Dr. Kamew was pretty out of touch with students;

the good professor was blatantly trying to humiliate Allen publicly in class. His mistreatment towards Allen, however, had the opposite effect. To the other students, Allen was a martyr. They came up one by one after class and spoke somberly and understandingly towards him as if a relative of his had died. He was another victim of how teachers never understood them. One young lady in particular wanted to express her compassion for the injustice done unto her fellow young, svelte student (for he was still laboring for Jimbo The Thing, also known as the Socratic Slave Driver, after class). She had noticed Allen, and he had noticed her. He had noticed her long brown hair, carefully coiffed to rise ever higher on the top of her head like a turban.

"Boy, that Kay-mew sure is a jerk. I can't believe he did that to you." She slouched familiarly, her books propped against the bottom of her Dallas Cowboys tee shirt, which stretched the fabric and accentuated her physique, which was considerably larger on top than in the middle or the bottom.

"Yeah, and the worst thing is I had read it. I just didn't know what it was supposed to mean. What in the world is propinquity?" Allen stared at the lettering on the tee shirt. He could only read "owbo." He realized he was staring and brought his eyes up to her face. "I mean, that's his job, isn't it? To explain it to us?"

"You're right. This stuff is hard, too." She swayed back and forth. "I bet his tests are really hard. Say, I have an idea. Why don't we study together? My name is Sharon, Sharon Mellon." She extended her hand to him.

"Yeah, that's a great idea," Allen said, shaking her hand very gingerly. She returned the shake smiling. Her smile seemed familiar as it finally clicked how he knew he recognized her. "You're the new Cob Queen, aren't you?"

"Yeah, that's me," Sharon said too bashfully. And that was how Allen met his second real love (or third, if you count the unseeing Karen, who had been far more to Allen in her own way than any woman he would ever actually make love to). As with most phenomena in our lives, familiarity brought knowledge. Allen found that with this second experience with romance came a greater feeling of control over the direction the relationship might take. (Of course, it was just a feeling for he had almost no control; he just didn't know that yet.)

In a sense, he owed it all to Dr. Kamew. But this romance was different from his romance with Beth Ann. This time, instead of disappearing from view by driving far out into the country, Allen and his love disappeared by being ever visible wherever there was disco music. Although Allen did not fancy himself a dancer, Sharon did consider herself one, and in truth she was a good enough dancer that it didn't matter that Allen was always a half beat slow. The two of them would dress up, her in a glittery, short dress and him in his stretch nylon shirt and double knit flared slacks, and they would disappear into the ranks of disco dancers at one of the four disco clubs in Evanston. As gaudy as they were, they were as invisible as if they had been transparent, for every other couple in the discos was dressed identically. Sometimes, they would even practice at Sharon's house before they went out. It was as if Sharon thought disco dancing was her ticket out of Evanston, that somewhere in one of the dark clubs with the flashing lights a movie director was waiting in the shadows awed by the scintillating grace of this dancing queen. She was sure to be whisked off to L.A. at any moment.

With the advent of this new romance, Allen felt less regret over the loss of his first love Beth Ann. Allen filled the void with his classmate Sharon. Meanwhile, Beth Ann had a torrid affair with her organic chemistry instructor. It's a funny thing about love affairs. The sour taste of the loss of one is only remedied by the sweet taste of another, like the way the taste of a rancid peanut can only be eliminated by eating another peanut that isn't rancid. Allen and Sharon danced and studied, in that order, for the rest of the semester and into the next year, and Allen became a better dancer primarily because he liked watching Sharon on the dance floor. It always excited him, and evidently her too, for they always ended up engaging in furious sex at the end of the evening.

This was another difference from Beth Ann. Being adolescents, Beth Ann and Allen certainly didn't let any opportunity pass them by (there is only the moment, for teenagers, and this moment might be the last). Beth Ann believed, for a short time at least, that she loved Allen, and the embraces they shared were always predicated on the tenderness that accompanies that sort of feeling. Sharon, on the other hand, was under no such illusions of love and went about her releases with a deliberateness and zeal that was all at once self-serving and reckless. All in all, Allen decided he liked the latter variety of passion better, even if he did have to admit to himself a certain emptiness in this romance.

Another curious thing occurred as well. After disappearing in the classroom failed, Allen decided the only way to survive college was by, of all things, studying. And despite the ill will Dr. Kamew felt toward him, Allen earned a C plus in the class and even took another philosophy class where he once engaged the professor in a lengthy discussion of the Socratic concept of techne and human excellence. Allen even tried to tie in the concept of a man's definition being inseparable from what he knows how to do based on his (almost daily) shop Socratic lessons— though they were more like monologues—taught by Jimbo. Like the time Allen tried to explain to Jimbo that it was senseless to wash the cars when heavy black clouds were blowing up from the horizon. "Ah'll tell you what, boy," Jimbo would say in response as he watched the large raindrops start falling on the still-wet-from-washing cars. "Warshin' dem cars is what we do. If'n we doan do what we do, we ain't what we are, we done lost ourselves, our defy-nition. Now you wouldn' wanna go t'rough life widdout no defy-nition, would ja?" Allen did not quote Jimbo in his discussion with Dr. Kamew, however, choosing to focus on the dialogue of Gorgias.

Thus in this first year of college, Allen had embarked on a new stage in his life, although he loathed admitting the changes. He had become a creditable student, surprisingly earning a solid B- average each of the first two semesters of community college. And the once invisible Allen became something of a social creature who was readily recognized by other disco dancers (though no one else would have been able to distinguish him from the rest of the tween trouser-wearing dancers). Even at the Ford dealership Allen had finally gotten noticed for his work and been promoted with an extra twenty cents an hour raise to a lot boy, who got to also work more with the new cars. Although, to be honest, it was probably as much due to the opening left when the previous lot boy had been sent to the state penitentiary for grand larceny when he was unfortunately implicated in a liquor store hold-up, but to Allen this was only the beginning of the kind of recognition that had been due to him all along. In his mind his plans, as nebulous as they had always been, were beginning to pay off.

But as he neared the start of his third semester of college life, Allen suffered some setbacks and grew impatient. At the community college, he suddenly felt as if he were another nameless face in a crowd of fifteen hundred nameless faces, taken for granted and unappreciated. Then just before the summer after his freshman year, Sharon had told him that she hoped they would always be friends but that she was not going to date anyone for several weeks while she tried to "get it all together," or something to that effect. The next weekend, Allen saw her stepping lightly with another young man with glittery pants, of all things, and perfectly combed hair that never became mussed even when he threw his arms up and head back in a kind of victory stance at the end of each song. (Allen secretly decided she left him because he couldn't speak Italian.) The day after that, Allen saw Beth Ann at the Dairy Drive-By, and she also told him that she hoped they would always be friends, for she and her agronomy professor were quite serious. She even confided that she thought she and the professor might have a future together once he left his wife, as she was certain he would. And, topping it all off, Jimbo had been put in charge of all the lot boys.

So Allen quit his job at Jimmy Jones Ford, packed his jeans and tee shirts and eight-track tapes, withdrew the two hundred forty-seven dollars and nineteen cents he had deposited in his savings, and announced to his family that he was moving to the city to go to the university. His mother looked directly at him but she didn't seem to see Allen. Instead she looked at him as if he were a little boy holding in his dirty little hands a math paper marked with a perfect score and a gold star. Teary eyed she hugged him, smiled slightly, and began humming a tune ever so softly. His little sister started measuring his room for her takeover. As for his father, well, his father looked at Allen with an expression partially misty-eyed, partially confused, and maybe a little bit angry, although Allen did not know what that was about. Then his father reached up, shook Allen's hand firmly, and said very seriously, if awkwardly, "Good luck, son. Write if you find time."

Allen felt very self-satisfied for a moment then pulled his father off to the side. "Uh, Dad, do you think you could help me out the first semester? I'm gonna stay with some friends and I've got enough money for books and such, but I need help with tuition and maybe with expenses later on."

Then all expression of anger and sentimentality left the face of the elder Mr. Johnson, and he had smiled broadly, slapped Allen on the back, and whispered, "You got it, son. Oh, and by the way, give it a ride, Allen." Allen rolled his eyes as he had since he was eleven.

So Allen left the invisibility of being a nameless, faceless community college student so he could shine forth as a sophomore at the university where twenty some thousand other young people were shining. Allen moved to live in a huge, drafty, ramshackle house with six other young men, none of whom had ever cooked or cleaned or even paid bills before. Of course they survived as young people are apt to. Allen ate primarily potato chips and soft drinks at first. Then moved to peanut butter, apples, and Kool Aid, and finally to slightly discolored bologna from Kroger's old meat bin and day-old bread from the bakery section. He was generally content with his lot. He didn't have a black light to go with his poster, but the music usually was quite loud, and there always seemed to be a party going on.

His father seemed to enjoy having a son at the university and sent him money occasionally. His mother even baked cookies and sent them through the mail, but if Allen wasn't at home when the package arrived, he never saw them. Every once in a while the Johnsons would drive to the city and visit Allen at the university. They would treat him to a meal at the Ponderosa and he would eat as if he hadn't eaten in a week, which was sometimes not too far off the truth. Other weekends, Allen would throw all his dirty clothes into the tiring Pinto and drive down to Evanston to visit his family and see Joey, who was now the Assistant Manager Trainee at Mario's.

In Allen's mind he was now a full-fledged college student, and he relished that. He was still a philosophy major, although he couldn't imagine what he might do with such a degree. He developed the habit of hanging around a local coffee shop where he usually drank water with a little lemon slice in it. There, he would dive into Kahlil Gibran, discussing the salient philosophical points with one of his classmates, or perhaps he would sit in the corner in a carefully unrehearsed pose reading Siddhartha and imagining the thrill of spiritual invisibility. He never went to discos now that he preferred to listen to obscure jazz musicians and the blues. He grew his hair longer, though not too long, and he wore blue jeans and tee shirts exclusively. All of that is to say Allen vanished, melted into the monolith that is higher education, and set his course on the path of erudition.

It should be noted, however, that Allen found no displeasure in this obscurity. Indeed, he never saw himself as anonymous. He was, after all, the hope of the future, right? As a college graduate, someday he would change the world. It all fit in nicely with his new tactics. He had been too late for protests and sit-ins, and the political world now seemed far removed from the academic world. There would be no contradiction in going from the university to business, although there was still the problem of his major to be considered. He once convinced one of his housemates, who himself was a business and finance major, that every business firm needed a resident ethicist to advise them in difficult situations, and his housemate suggested it to his business professor who guffawed at the thought of it. But Allen was quite satisfied as a college student, and as the semesters slowly melted away Allen grew more and more comfortable with his position.

Then something strange and terrible happened. One bright winter morning in 1980, Allen rolled out of bed and realized that he would finish college in less than three months. Oh, he had known that he would graduate that May for some time, but that particular morning it struck home that he would not be living in The Slum (as he and his friends lovingly, and accurately, called the house they shared), that he would need to get a job, and that he would even have to clean himself up in order to do that. It was quite troubling, for just when Allen seemed most comfortable in his situation, it was about to end. He tried to put it out of his head, but he couldn't shake the thought of going to a real job interview with a suit and tie and everything. Allen was depressed for three days until he and his friends pooled their resources and purchased two cases of cheap beer and drunk themselves into oblivion.

It is worth mentioning here that Allen saw all three of his former loves while he was a college student at the university. Sharon he saw on television dancing in the background while K.C. and the Sunshine Band mimed one of their songs on American Bandstand. In the middle of his sophomore year, Allen went to visit Beth Ann and they tried to rekindle their old love (unfortunately for Beth Ann, her agronomy professor had dropped her in favor of a graduate student who was sure that she had a future with the professor once he left his wife, which he was about to do any day now). The innocence of it all was gone, and the night had been forced and awkward. In the end, he kissed her on the cheek while she looked blankly at the ground and as they said "good night," they both understood it was really, "goodbye." Karen Dobroski, on the other hand, had also gone to Allen's university and had become a majorette with the band, was treasurer of the Pan Greek Society (a member in good standing of the Delta Delta Delta sorority), and was even elected to the student government, which didn't govern much, especially not the students. Allen saw her around campus still wearing ribbons in her blond hair. While he still felt a certain pang of lust and admiration, he also saw her as far too visible, even ostentatious, in her displays of self-promotion. He never engaged in reveries about her any more, though he certainly had many other classmates take her place in his perverse little daydreams.

Unlike in high school, Allen's desiring daydreams sometimes became realities, for he had garnered the attention of several co-eds around the university. He dated one after another and sometimes played a delicious, sometimes bitter, game of musical chairs with the young women he spent time pursuing. During his senior year at college, Allen engaged in a heavy romance with Carla Witherspoon, a quick-witted and fun young lady. She was from just across the river from Cincinnati in northern Kentucky, majored in elementary art education, and always knew when to laugh at Allen's witticisms. More importantly, and the primary reason for Allen's interest, was that she greatly appreciated, no, stood in awe of Allen's philosophical insights. He loved it when she told him that he was brilliant for his analysis of Berkeley's immaterialism, although he wasn't sure she had ever studied any philosophy. When she told him he was handsome, he expressed doubt but secretly admired her perceptiveness.

Throughout the fall and winter, Allen and Carla were inseparable. At the coffee house, they sipped Turkish coffee or water with lemon, depending on their budget, while discussing Kierkegaard's concept of the leap of faith (Kierkegaard's concept always brought Allen back to a sycamore grove for reasons he could not quite fathom). Or when all of Allen's housemates were chased away for the evening, they would sit intimately by candlelight in the filthy kitchen of The Slum eating Allen's self-proclaimed masterpiece, spaghetti marinara. A Chianti bottle (dripped with old crayons so that it looked as if a hundred thousand candles had been melted over the bottle) held the candle that cast a softening light over Carla's angular features and turned her otherwise drably brown hair an alluring auburn. Other times they studied in silence together and would take turns looking up appreciatively at the other. Or they would go to the campus theater and watch foreign films, most of which seemed more odd than art, but were at least foreign and therefore, by definition, intellectual. She read his papers and pronounced them "amazing" and "incredible." At times, she even pushed his hair out of his face when he was waking just to look approvingly at his just opening eyes.

Then, as the layers of snow began to give way to the March sun, Carla moved into Allen's room at The Slum, temporarily displacing James, a fellow philosophy major, who in the end had to approve the arrangement on philosophical grounds. Because he subscribed wholeheartedly to Nietzsche's theory of the Übermensch and where he came from, living together without benefit of marriage was a damnable sin. Carla and Allen agreed she wouldn't move everything into Allen's room, since her father was paying for her education and prudence required maintaining the semblance of still living with her girlfriends in another ramshackle house known affectionately, and accurately, as The Dump. But Allen felt very certain that she was living with him, and he embraced that she always, always noticed him. They were studious and devoted to each other in a manner Allen had not known he was capable of producing. And though Carla acted a bit shy around visitors to The Slum and even kept to herself when the other house mates (all male) were about, she changed character dramatically when the two of them crawled into Allen's creaky old double bed and exercised considerable imagination and energy to Allen's unending gratification.

At first, the advent of the creaks and groans of the tired bed were a source of embarrassment for Allen and Carla, and they engaged in various creative endeavors to enjoy their mutual love and lust without announcing it to the entire western hemisphere, but eventually they decided they didn't care who knew what and set about eliciting strange and wonderful sounds from the metal and wood of the bed. Sometimes, the housemates would claim Allen and Carla were grinding out their own rendition of "In-A-Gadda-Da-Vida," and the housemates would sit downstairs, swilling beer, and join in at the top of their lungs. "In-a-gadda-da-vida, Bayyybeee! Don't you know that I'm loving you!" Beer cans were flung against the wall. Allen and Carla laughed upstairs. Then Allen would fall asleep only to be awakened by his hair being brushed from his face.

This time when Allen graduated on an unusually warm May afternoon in the amphitheater of the university, mosquitoes swarmed the bastion of parents who were grateful and relieved that there were too many graduates to walk across a stage. Their beloved graduate would only stand for their recognition as "a graduate of the university with all the rights and privileges appertaining to" pronounced upon them by an Assistant Dean Trainee, or something to that effect, as if by magic. But before they would have their sheepskin mailed to them in three to four weeks (dependent upon final grades and whether or not all library fines had been paid), they had to endure their last lecture by an illustrious alumnus, Mr. Tresgrand. Mr. Tresgrand had gone on to become chairman of the board of a major clothier of mid-central Kentucky and now contributed generously to the School of Fashion Design. For his generosity, he received an honorary Doctorate of Fine Arts and was henceforth called Doc Tresgrand.

Doc Tresgrand had puzzled long and hard about his message and in the end had decided to speak analogously, taking as his image the ancient Chinese art of kite-making so that he could tell the future of America to "go fly a kite," as if that were some sort of wisdom.

It didn't really matter, of course, to Allen, because now he really was something; he was a college graduate, and all the twenty-two years of his life as a lot boy and a son and a student were about to be left behind. He was now a bona fide Bachelor of Arts with a major in philosophy. (He had written, for his senior essay, a treatise on the influence of Manicheans on modern Protestantism, with not one footnote to Rev. Pondermust's sermons on the subject when Allen and Beth Ann sat nervously in the pew.) Allen Johnson stood on the threshold of the world. He soon would exit the invisibility of academe and youth to embark upon the avenues of adulthood and commerce. And Carla, they had decided, would be at his side. (Perhaps they would not mention it to her father just yet.) She continued to read his papers, and her comments had moved from "incredible" and "amazing" to, "Does Descartes believe that dualism is one-directional? Your wording seems to say that here." But now Allen believed things were about to take off. In Allen's mind, he had been underappreciated for his entire life. He somehow didn't count the attention he took from his friends and Carla or even the occasional approving recognitions from the faculty in the philosophy department, including his advisor and semi-mentor, Dr. Easmane, known by his students as Dr. Easy Grade. But all of that was now over, for Allen was armed with a college degree, a woman, and the ability to transcribe fifty-minute monologues.

At long last, Allen Johnson was certain that he would be seen. He represented all that was wonderful and promising in the Class of '80. His plans for making an impact upon the world, impulsive and transitory as they may have been, were about to reap benefits, for Allen now stepped forth on the stage of life. Allen Johnson was on his own and determined to be noticed.

Cause and Effect

Life has a value only when it has something valuable as its object.
                                        -Georg Wilhelm Friedrich Hegel

Despite the lessons of substance and accident that college provided, Allen was ill-prepared for the transition into the next phase of his life. This phase involved the lessons of cause and effect, which were all the more difficult for Allen precisely because Allen still fancied that he was not the person defined by his circumstances. In his view, it was not the real Allen who now entered the work world with few skills and fewer prospects; the real Allen Johnson was formulating a philosophy of natural ethics that would revolutionize the world of philosophy in much the same manner his dreamt baseball skills had revolutionized the game of baseball. For learning life's lesson poorly, Allen was destined to pay a price, and it was only more painful because it was delayed. Everyone learns the same lessons; it's just better to learn them young. It's rather like Chickenpox that way.

Part of Allen's learning began immediately after college. Although he embarked on a path he was certain would lead to prominence if not fame and fortune, he had not planned on the events of the next few years and how the results would weigh Allen ever deeper into the pool of indistinctness. First, Allen decided that while being an adult was a grand maneuver towards being seen, working in an ordinary sort of job wasn't the best way to do that. Instead, Allen would use the vehicle of philosophy to make a name for himself.

So Allen put off trying to find a job as long as he could, intending instead to write that philosophical treatise on natural ethics and the pervasive human characteristic of fear of loss of sex (Hobbes had gotten it wrong, he decided; people didn't fear death as much as they did not being in bed with another person). He would write the definitive Freudian-Hobbesian ethics.

But since he and Carla were now intending to cohabitate, they could not very well just go and live with the Johnsons. Somehow, despite being braindead, his parents discovered Allen and Carla's living arrangements and told Allen they understood. In actuality, however, Mrs. Johnson couldn't figure it at all, and though Allen's dad understood, his understanding seemed jaded perhaps by what he remembered thinking about when he was Allen's age. He once pulled Allen aside, began stammering awkwardly about birth control, mumbled something about preventing diseases, but then stopped short. He turned and left the room suddenly while Allen stood there, his mouth agape, trying to decide whether that was the funniest or most bizarre episode in his life. The next day, a Planned Parenthood pamphlet saved from the early seventies appeared in Allen's suitcase. Allen folded it neatly, put it in his suitcase, smiled, and said a mental, "Thanks, Dad." Allen and Carla certainly couldn't go to live in the Witherspoons's home. Carla's parents, also braindead as all parents are, had not figured out the living arrangements. This was due less to a lack of knowledge but was more so simple denial that their precious little daughter could even have imagined such a thing. They certainly didn't know about Carla and Allen's personal "In-A-Gadda-Da-Vida."

With this in mind, Allen and Carla worked out a plan: each would go off looking for work, and the first one to find a job would send for the other. Allen went straight to Louisville, figuring that any city of that size would have considerable need for an ethicist, and though he may have been correct in that assessment, the Sunday Help Wanted section of the *Louisville Courier-Journal* listed no ads seeking an ethicist or even a philosopher. No one sought a humanist or a liberal artist or, for that matter, a well-read generalist. Everyone, it seemed, wanted a college graduate who could do something. They hadn't told him this at the university, and Allen was vexed.

Carla, on the other hand, called within the week to tell Allen she had found a position immediately at an elementary school in Covington (through some connections her father had at the school board) some fifteen miles from her parents' home. Allen was uncertain about it all, considering the proximity of her parents living nearby and everything else. But Carla assured him fifteen miles in northern Kentucky was as good as a hundred miles most other places, so Allen packed his jeans, tee shirts, eight-track tapes, and his one powder blue polyester suit, and he drove his rusting Pinto to Covington.

Once there, things began to move quickly. Allen and Carla surreptitiously set up house in a tiny, dingy apartment that was a part of the second floor of an old house. The space was so small that just to eat, their hinged kitchen table had to be raised in order to seat two. Later the table had to be lowered to open a passageway to the hallway which led to the bath, the largest room in the apartment. The landlady was an elderly, large, nosy woman who eyed Allen suspiciously when he and Carla signed the lease. But Allen explained that she had kept her maiden name after their marriage, and the landlady bought it and only shook her head in dismay at the youth of today.

Carla, on the other hand, gave a quick start when Allen said the marriage word, a word Allen had carefully avoided during all of their planning and scheming. But now he had said it, and back in their apartment Carla sat smirking on the corner of the hide-a-bed. Allen stood quizzically before her.

"What?" he asked with a smile to go with hers.

"Nothing." She sat smiling, her arms folded, looking quite satisfied.

"What? What's the joke?" His smile was more forced now.

"Oh, nothing, really." She waved him on, still smiling smugly.

"I don't get it. What's so funny?" His smile was fading now, and he stood closer.

"Nothing's funny." Her Cheshire smile hung before him. "I just thought it was interesting, is all."

"What? What are you talking about?" His smile was gone now, and he was a bit steamed by the riddle of it all.

"Oh, you'll see . . . someday. Someday." And it was clear she considered it dropped. Allen let it drop for now, although he couldn't help but notice subtle changes in their relationship, changes of which he did not disapprove. Carla became more diligent in her household duties she shared with Allen, often busying herself with them while Allen engaged in his studies. He would sometimes look up from his readings on philosophy of science (his new treatise on perception and the ethics of scientific change would revolutionize the world of science) and find her looking at him intently, but warmly, so that he felt at times a bit like a hamster in a box.

By the time two summers had rolled around, Allen found himself in a church in a rented tuxedo standing with Joey and James to one side of him. Allen supposed they were good for each other, and he was tired of checking out their window for Mrs. Witherspoon (she had dropped in unannounced once, catching the two of them lounging comfortably, both Carla's and Allen's clothes strewn about the place. The series of lies was shamefully transparent but eagerly accepted. She never dropped in again).

Allen's entire life was passing through his brain while Carla waltzed down the aisle in her grandmother's wedding gown, escorted by Mr. Witherspoon. There was something surreal about it all now, but Carla looked quite fetching. But as Allen stood patiently, he couldn't help but think about how Mr. Witherspoon was such a gigantic man with hands the size of cantaloupes and a testy personality. When it finally came time for Allen to say his "I do" and put a ring on Carla's finger, he collapsed into a heap before he could kiss his bride.

When Allen awoke, he could not figure out where he was. He could hear music in the next room, and he was lying on a bed somewhere with the faint odor of sachet clogging his olfactory. He sat up and then remembered that the reception was to be at Carla's Aunt Donetta's house. (Most of the nieces and nephews called her Aunt Donut which seemed appropriate considering her size, but Carla never called her that and was thus her favorite niece.) Then Allen realized that this meant he had actually gone through with it, and he was married. He wished he could faint again but couldn't, so he stood up and tried to make himself presentable. Had he really fainted in the front of the church before all those people? Allen looked at himself in the vanity mirror, and Carla peeked in at him. She had changed clothes, but of course Allen still had on his tuxedo, minus the jacket, so when she dragged him out of the bedroom, everyone was immediately reminded of Allen's faux pas at the church and began snickering about it. His baby sister Darlene (the reigning Cob Queen) even pointed and laughed. Yes, he must have actually fainted in the church. Why all his family and friends thought it was funny was beyond Allen. He had been noticed, at least, but that was small recompense.

Allen felt a wave of nausea as he walked out into the party. He wanted to go home to their new, slightly larger tiny apartment and go back to the good old days, but he knew those days were gone forever. Everyone was making a ruckus now, so Allen went in to the dining room and stood next to Carla where the photographer was motioning to him, and all the friends and relatives gathered about as she prepared to cut the cake. The last thing Allen wanted right now was cake, but that was not a problem since as soon as she had cut a piece, she smashed it into Allen's shocked face. He had heard of this odd ritual, but he had not anticipated it from his bride. He didn't like it—no, not one bit. Carla was pointing at him now and laughing, and Allen felt as if he were somehow far removed from this crowd. Now, everyone was pointing and laughing at Allen's face which had moved from shock to anger. Even the photographer snickered as he took pictures of Allen's fuming, icing-covered face, which Allen would later see as an interesting shot in tones of red and white. *So they think this is a real laugh riot*, Allen thought. Well, he decided he should get in on the laughs. He dug his hand into the cake, and just as Carla turned around to laugh at his expression again, he plastered the cake into her face. She looked quite surprised, but Allen somehow didn't feel much better. Now the guests were really hooting, especially Joey and James who were pointing at the blissful couple and slapping their sides. But Carla's eyes narrowed. Allen felt trapped, and his expression turned to confusion, which kept the guests rolling with laughter.

Finally, Allen could take it no more. He shoved both fists into the cake and threw huge chunks of cake at Joey and James. Then Allen grabbed more cake and threw wildly into the group before him. The reception broke into screams and scrambling feet. Joey was too far away from the cake to arm himself against Allen's missiles, so he reached into the platter of finger sandwiches and threw a handful of white bread and olive spread at Allen. Not to be outdone, James, in Nietzschean fashion, cupped his hands into the punch and started splashing it in Allen's direction, forever changing Aunt Donetta's white linen table cloth into a kind of tie-dye pattern of red and pink.

"Allen, stop! What are you doing?" Carla screamed. Allen froze. Joey nailed her with a finger sandwich on the forehead just above the icing line from Allen's wedding cake smash, the green canapé matting her bangs to her red face so that she looked quite festive, almost Christmas-like. "Joey," her voice was scarily calm now, and quite low. "If you throw one more sandwich," but she was too late, tiny pale mints showered her as "I will break your arm" escaped from behind her clinched teeth.

Joey looked at Carla's face and backed up toward the living room. There the other guests were peering around the corner and hiding, or grabbing car keys and huffing off into the hot summer sun, their suits and dresses painted gaily with punch and cake and various spreads from the sandwiches. "I'm sorry, Carla," Joey mumbled. "I forgot myself."

"That sounds like a wonderful idea. I think I'll try to do the same." Carla growled. Joey dashed out of the house, trailing cake and mints down the sidewalk. Carla whirled around to see Allen wrestling with James over a bowl of mixed nuts. "Allen!" He let go, and the nuts sailed across the dining room and peppered the wall like a spray of machine gun fire and settled into the cushion of a chair. "James! Stop it now!"

I'm in the Room

James was suddenly still. "I'm sorry, Carla. Allen started it." He pointed at Allen as he slowly edged toward the living room.

"No, I didn't. Carla started it!" Allen tried justifying.

"Allen." Carla's tone said it all.

"Well, you did." He interjected still futilely standing his ground.

James apologized, easing sideways around the edge of the room. "Really, Carla, I'm very sorry. I lost it for a minute, I guess."

"Uh huh." Carla's voice was slow and menacing.

James almost begging now. "Really, I'm so sorry, Carla. I'm so embarrassed by what I've done, I could just die, Carla."

Carla walked toward him. "Don't give me any ideas, James."

James ran from the room and out the front door leaving the coat to his rented tuxedo behind. Allen was alone now in front of the technicolored table, his sleeves covered in cake, punch dripping from his cummerbund onto the carpet that had once been pale blue but now was a mottling of colors. He looked at Carla and then at himself. The room was deathly quiet except for the sobs from Aunt Donetta in the next room.

"What have I done?"

"You've ruined MY wedding, Allen."

"Your wedding? It's my wedding, too."

"You just wouldn't understand, Allen. It's different for a woman. A wedding is a very special day, and it's supposed to be the best day in a girl's life. I somehow don't see that now." Carla was eerily calm.

"I'm really very sorry, honey. I don't know what came over me. Everyone was laughing at me, and my head started spinning and—"

"Heee haw!" Mr. Witherspoon screamed and suddenly a huge piece of the top layer of cake that had been removed before the fight started flew across the room spattering Allen's already icing-covered face.

"Daddy!" Carla screamed and ran from the dining room.

Allen groped for another piece of cake, but it was too late. "Heee haw!" Another piece of cake flew across the room and landed square on Allen's forehead. Allen stood meekly in the face of the salvage. "Heee haw." The last piece of the top layer lodged in Allen's ear. Allen reached for something, anything, to throw back.

"Don't you dare, Allen," Carla sniffed from behind the door where she sought protection.

"Heee haw." Carla's dad had picked up a pimento spread sandwich that stung Allen's cheek.

"Aiyeeee!" Allen howled.

Though Carla fumed for weeks about the spectacle at her reception (Allen dared not point out that at least he had not been yet another imperceptible bridegroom), she didn't pass up their honeymoon in Chicago. Although she wouldn't speak to Allen for the most part during the trip, they did manage to fulfill the remainder of their newly-wed responsibilities, so that two months later, Carla informed Allen that they were to be parents.

It all moved so quickly for Allen that he felt only marginally involved, except for the fact, of course, that he was forever affected. Only two and a half years ago, Allen had been a carefree college student with few responsibilities and fewer worries. Now, however, he was a husband with a child on the way. He had real responsibilities that he had always believed he would eschew. In other words, he was typical, and he hated that.

They were living almost exclusively off of Carla's income as a teacher, Allen being underemployed as a shoe clerk in a shopping center five miles and thirty minutes away from their apartment. Between the rent and the pay back from Allen's discovery of student loans midway through his sophomore year, they were pressed. So despite his misgivings, Allen gave up his avocation and vocation of lying around the apartment reading cookbooks and dreaming up new and ever more imaginative uses for ground beef and chicken wings. Allen daydreamed that his cookbook, *A Zillion Uses for Chicken Wings*, had become a monumental success, had sold millions of copies, and had been translated into fifteen languages. But since that wasn't coming to pass, Allen went back out on the job market and found a job as a collector for a local savings and loan. He considered his position to be one of enforcing the democratic ideals of America— why, somewhere in the writings of Jefferson and Locke was the dictum of the social contract and the individual's responsibility within the social order that ensues from that contract. One might even trace such ideals to the Iroquois League. Sure, collecting overdue loans was a link to the greatest traditions in European and American democracy and even the more obscure notions of Native Americans. Allen became rather good at lowering his voice and intimidating the late payers, most of whom were not deadbeats as his manager called them but folks who had borrowed money because they needed it and now that same need had returned. Nonetheless, Allen browbeat them and threatened to expose their slovenly ways to employers and family, or to garnish their wages (in democratic fashion). In the end, almost all of them found a way to repay the money that was owed.

In actuality, it bothered the philosopher in Allen that he was employed as an anonymous voice that threatened doom upon the hapless. Sometimes he worried that one of the debtors would somehow recognize him on the street and run over him with the very 1975 Lincoln purchased with the proceeds from the loan. Luckily, no one ever did and Allen was soon promoted to a desk position as the person who took the applications for the loans. He discovered that his job was to balance between benefactor and guardian. He was the kindhearted loan officer who could, if the customer groveled enough, convince the officers of the institution to approve the loan. In fact, the guidelines for approving loans were well established, and Allen knew immediately upon looking at a few of the spaces on the application whether or not it would be approved, but he maintained the illusion of power anyway. It would not do for the masses to understand the freedom that might be theirs. Allen was a kind of Grand Inquisitor, protecting mortgagees from economic salvation and the ills inherent in that salvation.

By the time another three years had passed, Allen was promoted to an Assistant Vice President Trainee in charge of second mortgages. Allen's son had been born, and Carla was pregnant again. They had moved out of their larger tiny apartment and had purchased, with five percent down, a lovely, thousand square foot cottage squeezed between two identical cottages in a subdivision squeezed in among the other subdivisions some twenty miles west of Allen's office so that Allen could drive forty-five or fifty minutes each way with the sun in his eyes.

Allen tried not to think about his life too much, but sometimes, especially late at night, the thought would occur to him that this was not what he had intended for his life. He was twenty-nine and still had not written that treatise on existential ethics that was sure to put his name on the lips of every free thinking adult in America. (He daydreamed he was on The Tonight Show and Johnny Carson announced the guests: "And on our show tonight, comedian George Carlin (pause for applause), singer Olivia Newton-John (pause for applause), and ethicist Allen Johnson (pause for thunderous and, yet, somehow, learned applause)." Golf swing and into the theme).

He also noticed that he had begun collecting cigar boxes, little pickle jars, and coffee cans (weren't they just perfect?), and that the child's crayons were in one particular basket while the colored pencils were in an old oatmeal box. The rubber bands went in a little jar that once held something they didn't use much, like capers, in it. Slowly but surely, the shelves in the closet lined up with containers. Allen also found he loved to be able to say to Carla, "Well, did you look on the shelf in the closet? There's a little box with a wooden handle on it that has several different kinds of glue in it. I'm sure you'll find what you need." Carla would always give him a smile that made him wonder if she ever needed the glue in the first place.

Allen thought about it one night and decided that he now knew why this change in his attitude had occurred, and why he now found his father coming forth in him. While maybe it was true when he was young that the world unfettered was a vast and glorious place, it was equally true now as an adult that that same world was chaotic and not just a little frightening at times. Allen read the paper and watched the news. So much of what was happening was beyond not only his control, but also, it seemed sometimes, the scope of his comprehension. It was a satisfying recourse, perhaps disproportionately so, that he could place just a bit of order in his life in a specific and finite way. He could sort out the tiny objects and place them in appropriate holders, and they would stay that way unless he changed them. He could create order out of chaos, and he asserted power over a portion of the universe, however small.

So now Allen eyed small bottles jealously and horded little odd-shaped boxes after Christmas so that he could further divide the tiny objects in the universe. But whatever comfort he took from this exercise in order, he could not erase the feeling that even the everyday events in his life seemed to spiral beyond his control, and every situation he found himself in was somehow created and defined by other people. Here he was, married to a nice girl, but he had never really thought about getting married. If someone had asked him to explain love, which was why you were supposed to get married (wasn't it?), he was not at all certain he could have done so. And then there was his three year old son, John Wesley Johnson, named after Allen's grandfather and Carla's great uncle. Was Allen ready for parenthood? He had done all the fatherly things: given out stale cigars with "IT'S A BOY" stamped on the plastic sleeves, bought his infant son a baseball mitt that would never be soft enough for a child to use and never be large enough for an adult to use, and his mother had come up to "help Carla" (trying to care for young John and keep Mrs. Johnson entertained very nearly wiped Carla out). His sister Darlene (who was now in her second year of medical school) had also come up with her husband, and they had ogled at the baby. Darlene had bugged her eyes at him and said, "Hesa bitty baby! Uh huh, he is! Hesa bitty baby! Uh huh!" And when he was old enough, John Wesley (as they called him) learned to say "da da" and later to say inappropriate things to guests at the house, which also endeared him to his parents (although later that habit would surely be a source of irritation for the Johnsons once he was a teenager). But in a sense, Allen felt as if it were happening somewhere else to someone else, and much too rapidly.

On Allen's thirtieth birthday, pregnant Carla waddled to the door, her arms full of crudely formed ceramic ashtrays her students had made, and pecked Allen on the cheek for what seemed like the zillionth time as he went out the door to drive to the "office" which was a desk in the middle of a room surrounded by other desks. His son had waved bye-bye as Allen had driven off but Allen had been looking the other way, towards something in the back of the house or on another planet or someplace further off than that. He drove absentmindedly without any notice of the passing vehicles to his "office." Once there, he dropped his briefcase, containing his lunch and a Sports Illustrated, and sat heavily in his sixties vintage swivel chair.

Allen's supervisor, Mr. Coldiron, the Associate Vice President in charge of residential loans, walked past without so much as a nod. Miss Prismire, the very old office secretary who had been at the savings and loan for some thirty years, also prissed past Allen's desk without a word. This was a bit surprising, considering that her frequent, personal espousals of the company were almost a daily thing. Alternating between the idea that the company was a bastion of hope and a giant of free enterprise (and thus she was a champion of capitalism), or that the company was a pit where the scum of the earth visited to somehow escape the responsibilities of thrift (and thus she was a pawn in the heartless usury of her fellow Americans). Never had Allen felt more lost, and it weighed him down tremendously.

Allen sat for a long time, staring off at nothing until he heard the guard, an octogenarian with a blue uniform and a can of mace, jingling his keys toward the front door to unlock the gates for the impoverished horde to enter. Allen thought about his day. He would read forms and shake hands and sit across his desk from dozens of people today, and not one of them would be able to later describe to their friends and relatives the loan officer they met today. Whether they received the loan or not, he would still be anonymous, it made no difference. Depositors would walk into the lobby and never look beyond the brass railing that divided the business into the tellers and the loan department. Then later, Carla would ask him what happened this day, how it went, who he met, to which he would only be able to shrug and say, "Nothing," the same way he had responded for years to his parents' similar questions about school. He was a mere drop in a very placid, forgettable lake. Allen couldn't stand it anymore. No sooner had the ancient guard been able to jiggle the door lock open than had Allen picked up his briefcase, put his three photographs from his desk in it, and walked out. Allen walked to the blacktop sea where his battered Pinto awaited, threw his briefcase in back, and drove off for home to see John Wesley, and, more importantly, be seen by John Wesley. And as he drove off, he felt suddenly and overwhelmingly free, and that freedom sent his head into a whirl of confusion.

Reciprocity

Man is the only animal that can be a fool.
-Holbrook Jackson

As Allen went about discovering the results of his actions, he found that he could cause things to happen and that he could simultaneously be affected by actions beyond his control. What he had not yet discovered was that none of these actions occurred in a vacuum. All actions in Allen Johnson's life were interconnected in a kind of fabric of choices and decisions made by and about him, or sometimes without the subject realizing that an Allen Johnson ever existed. Such was the case with his decision to leave his position at the savings and loan.

Allen was surprised at the various reactions his unannounced departure received. The savings and loan didn't call for four days, apparently not noticing for at least three days that the Assistant Vice President Trainee of Second Mortgages was missing, and then discovering that, for one day anyway, the results had been negligible. When Miss Prismire had called, Allen told her that Mr. Johnson wasn't home but had been taken off to the Home for the Morally Insane, which brought only a long, icy silence from the other end of the line and then a terse, "Thank you."

When Allen called James at the university where he was in the fourth year of his master's degree program, James laughed at the tale and told him that it was the first ethical decision Allen had made in years. Allen had created for himself an opportunity to transcend the mundane, to excel; he had made a wonderful wager on life. By having cleaned the tablet, Allen now knew more than anyone else could have ever told him, and James was quick to point out that, as Dewey had noted, it wasn't how knowledge is achieved that is important but that one achieves knowledge at all. When he hung up the phone, Allen had a terrific headache and whirring, mixed images of Nietzsche, Bacon, Pascal,

Dewey, and Grandpa. Allen understood now why James still had several years to go on his thesis.

Carla had not been so understanding as James had been. She had furrowed up her brow beneath her bangs and said quite halfheartedly, "Well, honey, if you don't want to work there at the bank, maybe Daddy could use you in his construction job." She was a devious one, that Carla, even if she wasn't all that subtle. Now of course Allen knew this was said to send him scampering off to the savings and loan to beg for his job back, but Allen only scoffed at her manipulations.

"No, I've got a better idea. Let's run off to Colorado and join a commune."

"Oh, Allen," she giggled, "you're so funny. I mean really, what are you going to do if you don't work at the bank?"

"I'm serious, Carla. Let's just take off and live in the wilds and maybe eat trout from the stream cooked over a fire you made by rubbing two sticks together."

"I don't like fish. You know that. And I'm taking a book of matches." She responded still thinking it was all a joke.

"Great! You get the baby. I'll grab our sleeping bags and some canned goods." Allen plunged into the closet searching for the camping materials. When he did, he banged his head on his shelf of tiny boxes and jars, tipping them over and emptying their contents to the floor of the closet. Allen froze for a moment, his head caught in a shower of little nails and screws and rubber bands and paper clips. He stood up slowly and looked at the chaos on the floor.

"Allen, now really," Carla had a broad grin of amusement, "what is it you want to do if you don't want to work at the bank? I really could call Daddy and ask him if he needs anybody."

"You're not listening, Carla." Allen turned and faced her, his face feeling very hot. "I don't want to work at the 'bank,' as you insist on calling it, and I certainly don't intend to work for your father. I want to get out of here. I've got to get someplace where I can do what I need to do. I want to break out. I'm tired of being insignificant and purposeless. I need to write that treatise."

"You need to have your head examined is what you need to do. What's the matter with you? We don't have it so bad, do we? We've got a house, a beautiful baby and another on the way." She said the last part very loudly and patted her melon-shaped abdomen so that, as Allen saw it, there was no mistaking that Allen had responsibilities.

"But look at us, Carla." Allen was up and pacing the tiny kitchen. He caught his reflection in the toaster oven; his face was bright red. "We never go anywhere, we never do anything, and we never see anyone. This life? This is the only shot we've got. Let's not throw it away on a meager existence like this. We never do the things we used to do."

"We aren't the people we used to be, Allen." Carla rubbed her belly uneasily.

"What?" Allen snapped back.

"Allen, I think you are a smart and good man, and I know you want to make a difference. But you make a difference for me, and for John Wesley, and for lots of other folks, like the people you help get loans at the bank. Is that bad?" She was pleading with him now.

"I never worked at a bank. And the fact is, we don't have any fun anymore." He could tell his words stung as Carla looked at the floor. "I don't mean it that way, honey. I mean, we don't even have sex more than the minimum twice a week that's required by law."

"Now Allen, not in front of the baby." Carla's tone hardened now.

"In front of the baby? We don't have sex in front of ourselves!"

"Allen! Stop that!" Carla's voice shook a little. "You're starting to scare me."

"Stop what? Now kinky sex is leaving the light on," Allen yelled.

"Allen, please. The neighbors—" Her eyes flickering to the window.

"You want to invite the neighbors over to watch? That's a great idea!" Allen was screaming now at the top of his lungs. "They can watch and maybe join in with 'in-a-gadda-da-vida, honey. Don't you know that I'm loving you?'" Allen did a bump and grind across the kitchen. "Mrs. Bunhead next door probably has a great voice. In-a-gadda-da-vida, baby." Allen directed a few pelvic thrusts at the window.

"Allen, stop that!" Carla looked like she couldn't decide whether to laugh, slap some sense into Allen, or run out the door with little John Wesley and let Allen go completely mad. She opted for pulling down the shade on the window.

"What, d'you really think that's gonna stop me from telling this petty little world full of petty little people thinking ridiculously petty little thoughts what I think? Ha!" And Allen ran out the front door onto the tiny porch of their tiny home to the vision of everyone on the block standing on the sidewalks in front of their houses or next to the street, straining to listen to Allen's tirade. One especially adventurous woman was even standing at the edge of Allen and Carla's yard in the grass. Now their task was far easier. Allen had never before been so visible. He addressed his congregation. "So what d'ya think, folks? This was what we were born for? We're born to get stinking little jobs for stinking little pay checks so we can live in these stinking little houses in stinking little subdivisions in—in stinking Kentucky?"

"Give 'em hell, Allen," one brave old man shouted. His wife elbowed him hard in his ribs, and he doubled over and dragged himself back into his house. Everybody else only stood staring with a sense of wonderment at which particular frustration had caused this man to snap.

"Allen, please." Carla stood on their tiny front porch and tugged at his sleeve with one hand and rested her other hand on her midsection.

"Please? Please? I am not pleased. No, not one little bit. I am greatly displeased over the course of our lives." He was lecturing to the neighbors now, waving his arms about and posing for Mrs. Bunhead. "Are you pleased with the course of your life, Mrs. Bunhead? Is this life everything you thought it would be?" Mrs. Bunhead stood there silently, her lips pursed tightly. "Well, Mrs. Dickhead? Have you read the assignment? Have any of you read the assignment? Are any of you ready for the exam? Because it's here. It's test time, Mrs. Scumhead." Allen was out in the yard now, waving grandly.

"My name is Bimstead, Mr. Johnson," Mrs. Bunhead finally answered haughtily.

"Wrong answer, Bonehead! You fail. Aiyee! Anyone else care to try?" Allen paused for an answer and suddenly felt very alone. The neighborhood was deathly quiet except for Carla's sniffling from the doorway. Allen had a strong sense of déjà vu. Carla stood behind the door caressing her great mid-section. Her eyes were red with anger, fear, and confusion. Allen stopped in his preacher-like pose and looked about at the faces of his neighbors, still and gaunt and full of fear and disbelief. No one said a word. Finally, Allen decided to end the silence. "No one? Okay, class dismissed." Allen ran back into the house and slammed the door.

"Oh shit," he said when the echo of the door had faded, "what did I just do?"

"Well, off hand, I'd say you just showed your ass in front of the entire neighborhood." Carla stood with her arms crossed, her face contorted with anger and sorrow. "What in the world is wrong with you, Allen?" She raised her hand to her eyes to catch a tear.

"I'm sorry." Allen shook his head as if to try to erase what just happened. He gathered his wits and looked at Carla and her pregnant midsection and felt a sharp pang. He looked back at her moist eyes. "But I'm telling you the truth when I say let's get out of here."

"Well, I'd say that's a good idea," Carla waved her hand towards the door, "now that you've alienated the entire street."

"Aw, those people are already so alienated they don't know which end is up. To tell the truth, I don't care what they think." He shrugged.

"That seems pretty obvious. What about what I think?"

"Honey, I need to get away for a while." Allen held Carla's arms in his hands.

"Oh, really? I thought maybe you were wanting to buy a red sports car and grow a mustache and maybe start wearing a gold chain and have a fling with a little co-ed named Bambi."

"No. No. I just need to get away for a few weeks."

Carla swatted him. "I was kidding, dammit. You're supposed to say, 'I'd never have a fling with anyone but you, Carla my sweetest.' You are off your rocker, Allen Johnson. Go on, get away. Go somewhere. I've had it with you."

"Yeah, maybe I will. That's a good idea, honey." He said as his face began to lighten back up.

Carla stared at him in disbelief. "Don't make this sound like my idea."

"Oh, yeah. I guess that was me." Allen wandered back to his room to pack some things.

Outside, everyone was buzzing. That young banker fellow had seemed like such a nice young man. Everyone wondered why he had become so strange all of a sudden. Three third graders on bicycles rode past the house next door and called out, "Hey Mrs. Dickhead, d'you study for your test?" They circled around in the street like a pack of wolves baiting the old elk to charge into the underbrush. "Dickhead didn't study. Dickhead didn't study." They sang in unison. The other adults snickered, and finally the mother of one of the boys shooed them off. Slowly, the neighbors drifted off to their homes, and more than one husband sang softly to his wife that night as they snuggled close in their beds, "Dickhead didn't study. Dickhead didn't study." Poor Mrs. Bimstead was henceforth referred to by that ignominious name whenever the neighbors gossiped about her son in the Navy who no one had ever seen date a girl but was probably cozy on one of those big ships with all those cute fellows, or so they speculated and mocked. Occasionally, someone would even slip up and call her that to her face, but she always acted as if she hadn't heard. Meanwhile, her son flew jets over Iraq.

Allen Johnson grabbed his old duffle bag and threw things in haphazardly. He ended up with twenty pairs of underwear, three pairs of socks and four other socks that had no mates, eight tee shirts, his baseball mitt, a tired but still functioning Zebco rod and reel with knotted line on it, four faded yellow legal pads on which he had written notes for his treatise, a couple of ball point pens from a candidate for public office, and a half dozen battered cans of Vienna sausages from an aborted fishing trip with James the previous summer. Allen had packed no pants and no shoes other than those on his body. He threw a sleeping bag into the back seat and went up to Carla.

"Honey, I'm sorry I acted so badly," he said holding her hands, "I just need some time to sort things out."

"Where in the hell are you going?" She glowered at him.

"I'm going to Colorado to fish for trout and write a book." He answered innocently.

"What? No, you're not." She tightened her grip on his fingers, "You're going to your parents' house and see Joey and get away for a few days, and then you're going to call me and we're going to talk."

"Actually, that was my next choice." He forced a smile.

"And call me when you get there so I'll know you're okay," still tightening her grip.

"Yes, dear." So Allen Johnson kissed Carla and patted her stomach as pregnant women love for folks to do, and he kissed John Wesley on his head. He walked slowly to his car now on the deserted street (it was almost ten o'clock). He pulled the groaning door of the Pinto closed and drove off. He had really thought that Colorado was a grand idea, but just driving off anywhere was better than nothing. Before long, Allen was sailing down the highway, singing with the radio and feeling as unfettered and visible as he had imagined he could. He was, in a sense, for the first time, living out his dream of going his own way, of being the master of his own destiny, of being in charge. He didn't have to go to work tomorrow because he didn't have a job anymore. Maybe he and Joey could go fishing in the river. He could stay up late writing the quintessential masterwork on the American philosophical psyche and then sleep until noon if he wanted. It was grand just thinking about it, but before he was half way to Evanston, he was missing Carla and wondering what John Wesley would wear the next day to daycare.

When he arrived at his parents' home, Carla had called ahead, and his mother was waiting up for him with a plate of macaroni and cheese and a cubed beef patty, medium rare. (Allen very nearly burst into tears at the sight of what had always been his favorite meal.) He called Carla then went upstairs to what had been his room since he was six.

Allen came into the room and discovered his bedroom had been converted into the room for his father's new hobby of model railroading.

Allen turned on a train, and watched it chug slowly around the track until it neared a street crossing, and a miniature crossing gate began flashing as the gate lowered. Allen turned off the train and sat for a long time, looking at the tiny people stuck on the plastic buildings and frozen on the papier-mâché hills. The people were neatly arranged and carefully posed so that some of them were forever picking up a load at the minuscule lumber yard, or perhaps terminally engaged in fishing from a tiny dock in a glass pond under a spongy tree. Allen remembered Dr. Easmane talking about Camus and telling the students how Sisyphus's punishment was not pushing the rock up the hill, but watching it roll back down, the effort wasted, the task to be futilely repeated forever. These tiny people never suffer, thought Allen, because they never have time to reflect on the futility of their lives. It was the closest Allen came to the Flying Leap until fourteen months later, when quite consciously Allen Johnson would become completely invisible. Allen turned off the light in his old room and went back down to the basement. There awaited the pull-out sofa bed with the bar across the back that he knew would leave him stiff and miserable the next day. He stripped to his undershorts as he had always slept when he lived in this house and promptly fell asleep.

Essence

Lots of people know a good thing the minute the other fellow sees it first.
                                              -Job E. Hedges

Allen awoke the next morning at six, the time he always got up so he could help get John Wesley ready and still get into town before eight. He tried to roll over and fall back asleep, but the ache in his back met the bar in the mattress and Allen decided to go ahead and get up. He carefully folded up the bed and dressed, discovering the short comings in his packing but deciding it didn't matter. He was retired. Yeah, that's it. Allen was retired at thirty. Now that had a nice ring to it.

Allen went up to the kitchen and made a pot of coffee, sprinkling some cinnamon on the grounds as a special treat. While he waited for the Mister Coffee to heat the water and run it through the grounds, Allen retrieved the paper and spread the sports page out in front of him on the table. His mother floated into the room in her night gown, a pink quilted floor-length model, and with her hair already brushed. She hummed softly to herself as she brought down three cups from the cabinet, one that said "MOMS ARE GREAT" that Darlene had given her, another that had a print of a train on it, and another that was solid white except for the web of cracks that ran down the sides. She poured a cup for herself and one for Allen and sat across the table from him. She looked at Allen with a soft, worried look that she had practiced for years on her husband. She took a sip of her coffee pensively.

"Oh!! Oh dear, the coffee's gone rancid." She jumped up from the table. She then grabbed both cups and the coffee pot, and before Allen could explain, she dumped it all down the sink. Starting another pot, she hummed softly while sniffing in bewilderment the coffee can that would later be used to hold pencil erasers that her husband would saw off the end of used up pencils. He would paint the erasers black to look like miniature oil drums that a miniature man would stack forever next to a miniature sand and gravel company.

"Is Dad up?"

"He'll be down in a minute. He's quite concerned about you, Allen. I tried to explain things to him." Allen's mother had portrayed herself as the children's ally for as long as Allen could remember, but Allen always suspected she was not as loyal to them as she wanted them to believe. It had been his mother, after all, who had Darlene when Allen was five. "I must say, Allen, I don't much understand it all myself."

"It's okay, Mom. Things will work out. You'll see."

"Well, I hope so. But I just don't understand why you would quit a wonderful job at a bank like that when you have a lovely wife and little John and a baby on the way."

"It wasn't a wonderful job, Mom, and it wasn't a bank, for that matter, and besides, I have no intentions of leaving my family out on the street like waifs or something the way you make it sound. As a matter of fact, when I get done we'll be rich and I'll be famous, and Carla and the kids will have a better life than they ever dreamed they would have." His mother was pouring them coffee. "You know what else, Mom? I was meant for better things than to push paper across a desk for eighteen thousand dollars a year. I went to school and I've paid my dues and now I'm ready for bigger things, more important things."

Allen's father came slowly into the room, his face tired and older looking than Allen remembered. "Well, what is it you want to do, son?" He scuffled over to the coffee pot and poured his train cup full.

"Well, I've got some ideas, but I'd rather not say just yet. I don't want to jinx myself or anything. You know what I mean, Dad?"

His father turned around and scuffled slowly to the table. He did not look at Allen. "Uh huh, I do know what you mean. You mean you don't have a clue what you're going to do and you don't want to admit it."

"No, that's not it at all!" Allen slammed his hands against the table and jumped up. "You just wouldn't understand."

"Well, I never have," Allen's father shrugged, "why should now be any different?"

"You just wait and see. I'm going to do something important, something great, and then you'll see." Allen yelled like a petulant child. "I've got big plans, you just wait and see." Allen stomped up the steps to his old room, wondering why his father could see right through him. Allen was almost to the door of his room when he remembered that it wasn't his room anymore and his dramatic exit had been for nothing, and now he would have to slink past his parents who would be smirking at him as he skulked back down to the basement to get his things.

Allen called Joey, whom he hadn't seen since the free-for-all at the wedding, to see if he wanted to go fishing, but Joey had become the Regional Manager of Mario's Inc., a multinational corporation that shipped restaurant supplies and processed foods around the world, and also ran Mario's Pizza Emporiums, a chain of three hundred pizzerias throughout the Midwest. Joey was in charge of a two and a half state area, he informed Allen, and was pulling down forty thousand dollars a year plus a car and an expense account. Joey couldn't go fishing because he was training a manager at one of the pizzerias in the next county. Allen hung up the phone in a pique, not because Joey couldn't go fishing but because Joey was doing so well in spite of having never gone to school, indeed, perhaps because he didn't quit his job and go to school. It just didn't seem fair to Allen.

Allen tossed his Zebco into his Pinto and cranked the engine for several minutes until it finally rumbled to life. The trusted old car was definitely on its last legs and there was no way for Allen to replace it. Allen decided that maybe Jimbo, The Thing—who had actually been something of a whiz when it came to used cars, now that Allen thought about it— could fix his old Pinto for old times' sake. It felt odd, somehow, driving down Frederickston toward the car dealership where Allen had held his first job. The streets looked pretty much the same, the traffic lights were out of sync as they had always been, and even the pot holes were where Allen had remembered them, although he decided that perhaps these were new pot holes replacing the former pot holes as if there was no repairing these cursed spots. The entire town of Evanston was probably built on an ancient Native American burial ground, the curse of which was a rejection of asphalt.

Turning the corner at Ninth Street, Allen was greeted by the familiar old garage with the same glass façade and the same empty lot next door where Allen had burned the trash. His cousin Louis was still there, though he was now the Used Car Manager (his father had informed him as he stomped around the basement this morning). But one thing was very different. Instead of the huge fading sign that had declared this territory for Jimmy Jones Ford there was a new, bright green sign that informed the world that this was Jimbo's Ford-Lincoln-Mercury and A-1 Pre-Owned Cars.

Allen's chin dropped and his foot hit the brakes so hard that the Pinto stalled in the middle of the street. Allen stared at the sign while he cranked the now moribund engine. The smell of gas filled the car and Allen realized he had flooded the engine. He put the car in neutral and got out to push the car to the side. His eyes were fixed on the sign the entire time. Allen's brain however seemed completely unwilling to process this piece of information. Finally, his cousin Louis came trotting out to help push the dead Pinto, not realizing it was Allen but seeing a golden opportunity to sell a clunker to a needy pedestrian. When he saw it was Allen, he considered returning to the showroom, but instead shrugged and pushed the rusty vehicle to the curb.

"Thanks, Louis." Allen panted, still staring at the sign. "Is that the same Jimbo . . . ?"

"Oh yeah, that's Jimbo all right. You didn't know he had bought out the old man? Seems Jimbo's been living out in a corner of the garage and saving his money, and when the dealership hit hard times in the embargo he bought the whole thing. Paid cash for it, they say. I don't doubt it. You should see the way he dresses and his car. Man, what I wouldn't give for a town car like that." Louis could see the expression on Allen's face, a mixture of disbelief and bewilderment. "Don't sell him short, Allen. Seems he's got quite the head for business and he really knows people. Every Monday he gives a little inspirational speech to the sales crew and we actually look forward to it. I've even gotten to the point where I use what he says with my own kids. Like, for instance, one of his favorite things to say is, "You've got to believe in yourself. A man is—"

"What he does," Allen finished the sentence. "Yeah, I remember." His mouth was still hung open. "Inspirational talks? A head for business? This is really more than I can stand. This is incredible."

"What's the matter, Allen? Why do you care? What, are you jealous that old Jimbo's done so well? He worked hard, saved his money, and now he's made a name for himself. Why, he's one of our civic leaders now. Haven't you seen his ads on TV? He does all his own ads."

"The Thing is on TV?" Allen screamed. "He's a civic leader?" Allen waved his arms and began to pace up and down the sidewalk next to his broken down Pinto. "I can't believe this. This is absurd. Here I've gone to college and I'm working in some penny-ante job and Jimbo the Moron is running Evanston." Louis stared at his ranting cousin. Allen looked to the heavens for some indication of the injustice of it all when a long, sleek, black and silver Lincoln Towne Car glided past where they stood. Allen

I'm in the Room

froze in horror and stared at the huge, expensive vehicle that was stopping in front of them. A window in the back seat of the car glided down and Jimbo the Moron pushed his red crew cut through the opening.

"Is dat one of dem lot boys what we useta had workin fer us?"

Louis stepped lightly to the side of the car. "That's my cousin Allen. Remember him? He worked for us for about a year before he went off to school. You remember. Went to the community college." Allen stepped up to the vehicle as if he was receiving an audience with the pope. "Allen, you remember Jimbo, don't you?"

"Uh, yeah, I mean, yes sir." Allen extended his hand for a benediction. Jimbo took his hand and Allen felt a sharp pain shoot up his arm and down to his knees which buckled. Jimbo let go of his hand and shook his head as if Allen had failed the test again.

"Doan ever give a man a wet fish, boy," Jimbo advised as Allen rubbed his squashed palm and stared at the hulking figure sitting half out of the car window, a staid driver sitting in the front staring forward and not wavering in his demeanor. Allen looked at Jimbo with an expression of amazement. "Whatsa matter, boy? You look kinda sick. Oh, I git it. Yore jest like de rest o' dem folks. You cain't believe dat ol' Jimbo done well for hisself. Well, it di'n't come easy, no sir. Ah saved and scraped fo' everyting ah got. I'll tell you what, son. When a man knows de virtue in thrift, he is virtuous, and de thrift'll come as a natural rezult o' dat knowledge. Ah paid mah dues, boy." And with that, Jimbo pulled his head in and waved the driver on toward the dealership. Allen stood there in disbelief.

"He reads Socrates," Allen mumbled. "The Thing has a chauffeur and he reads Socrates."

Louis looked at him evenly. "His name is Jimbo Fuller, Allen, and Jimbo can't read. I thought you knew that."

"What? Aiyeeeee!"

Subjective Notion

Fishing is the chance to wash one's soul with pure air. It brings meekness and inspiration, reduces our egotism, soothes our troubles and shames our wickedness. It is discipline in the equality of men - for all men are equal before fish.
-Herbert Hover

Allen finally cranked up the tired Pinto and rumbled off away from the car lot. His head was hot and he had fuzzy visions of Joey and Jimbo and how everyone else seemed to be doing famously despite what Allen perceived as their debilitating flaws. Jimbo was an idiot who may have been slated for institutionalization, except that he probably massacred his family with a double-sided ax when he was four. And Joey, his best friend Joey, who no longer had time for the petty inconveniences of his buddy Allen, whom Allen had seen eat a Japanese beetle once on a dare, was making a killing in the restaurant business despite having no education (high school certainly wasn't an education) and despite having been a virgin until he was twenty (actually, Allen couldn't figure why that should matter, but as long as he was on a mental tirade he might as well add it to the list). Allen bounced down the road that he had travelled so many times as a younger man seeking solitude, first with Beth Ann and later with Sharon.

His hands held the steering wheel tightly (although his right hand still ached from Jimbo's crushing handshake), and his focus was on the farthest point up the road where he was headed. The daffodils grew in clumps along the side of the road and the trees were bright green with new growth. But Allen didn't notice. He was bound to go fishing and he was headed for the river. Allen drove for a quarter of an hour until the road suddenly forked and one road, not much more than a path really, led off to the left, and the other wandered on up the hill and then down next to the river. Allen parked the Pinto, grabbed the beat up fishing pole from behind the driver's seat where it had rolled, and made his way down the bank to the edge of the river. The narrow bank was rocky and covered with pebbles, and it seemed distantly familiar to Allen. The river made a soothing, constant rush over the rocks. Allen reached into his shirt pocket and pulled out the rusting red and white spoon he had found in the basement of his parents' house. He tied the spoon on with a mixture of some knots he had seen once in an old book on fishing and the kind of knots he made inadvertently in his tennis shoe laces. He pushed the button on his Zebco and threw his arm in a wide circle, spiraling the lure far out into the water.

Something about reeling in the lure, the cool of the water, and the constant low roar of the water punctuated by the calling of robins and cardinals soothed the fierceness in Allen's head. He slowed down to a more gradual retrieve on the lure (he realized that he had been reeling so fast that the lure was skimming along the top of the water. He started casting up and down the river, first upstream, then downstream, then straight out from him. He still had not gotten a bite so he decided that maybe his retrieve was still too fast. He started cranking very slowly and felt a hard tug on his line. He jerked back sharply on the pole, locking in the hooks. Allen tried to reel, but the Zebco only let out a plaintive whine and Allen realized the lure was stuck not on a fish but on an unseen obstacle somewhere deep in the water. He yanked on the line, but it wouldn't budge. He pulled hard on the pole to try and break the line, but it held firm. The fifteen-pound test was kinked and knotted, but it was still tough. He yanked again—nothing. Allen shook with frustration. It was the same old story. He yanked and pulled on the line, but it wouldn't move. Allen dropped his rod on the bank in disgust.

"If you walk up the edge of the river, it'll come out of its own accord." Startled, Allen whirled around, for he hadn't heard the footsteps behind him. Standing there was a short, squat woman with a lumpy, pale face holding a couple of fishing poles and a small box in one hand and a bucket in the other. "Here. Lemme show you." She carefully put down her own tackle and picked up Allen's rod from the ground. She walked up the river about thirty feet and the lure pulled out from the rock. She reeled in the line, and laughed while looking at the rod. Handing it back to Allen, she held the rod away from her as if it might have some sort of germ on it. "This here is a genu-ine antique, idn' it?" She laughed.

"Yeah." Allen took the rod and nodded, "I've had it since I was a kid."

"Same line, too, huh?" She shook her head.

"Uh, yeah. Are you supposed to put new line on it?" Allen stared at the fiberglass pole in his hand.

The woman picked up her tackle and positioned herself on a large rock beside the river. "You're no expert on fishin', are you? Yeah, you gotta replace the line every now and again so's it won't get all balled up while you're pullin' in some lunker." Allen watched her carefully as she pulled line from one of her reels and threaded it through the eyelets of a fishing pole. She carefully twisted the line in some mysterious knot that Allen couldn't begin to imitate and groped in her bucket for some bait. "You got a sinker?"

"Nah, I mean, no ma'am." Allen kicked some pebbles aimlessly, embarrassed at his lack of prowess at fishing.

"Here." She reached out her hand and gave Allen a heavy egg-shaped piece of lead and a large hook. "Tie this on about eight inches up then tie this on the end." She had a calm, coarse voice that Allen recognized vaguely. Allen took the gifts and set about wrestling with the stiff fishing line on his pole. He cut the spoon off with a little pen knife he had retrieved from the train room at home and tried to imitate the knots he had seen the woman tying. The woman watched him with a look of mild bemusement until she evidently couldn't take it anymore and broke into a hearty laugh. Allen felt his head getting hot again. She took the pole from Allen's trembling hands.

"Here, son, lemme show you somethin'." Unlike the jumbled knots Allen had made, she tied a concise little knot on the weight and another knot like a miniature hangman's noose around the hook. "There. She's all set."

Allen held the line in his hand and stared closely at the set up the woman had tied for him. She handed him a large night crawler and threaded one on her own hook. "Like this, son." And before Allen could tell exactly what she had done, she flipped the end of the rod and the weight sailed out into the river. The line settled, pulled downstream, and finally pulled tight with the current. Allen struggled with the worm, then finally when he felt ready, threw his arm in a wide circle, the weight and hook twirling out into the river. He let it settle like he had seen the woman let hers settle. They sat on a log together. He watched her carefully out of a corner of his eye, but she only sat and gazed noncommittally at the river. Finally, Allen felt a pull on the line, then another and then suddenly the pole was twitching violently. Allen watched and then realized what was happening and pulled back hard on the pole. Now the pole came alive with jerks and steady pulls and whining line as the fish pulled up, then downstream to escape the hook in his mouth. Allen stood next to the water now and reeled steadily until the blue-grey catfish was lying on the gravel at his feet, gasping. When he looked down at the fish, he heard the rush of the water over the rocks, realizing that he had been yelling at the top of his lungs as he caught the fish, and now the woman was guffawing over his excitement.

"That's a right good channel cat, son," she managed to get out between chuckles. Allen stood there sheepishly, chagrined over his amateurish behavior, but still very pleased with his fish. He picked up the fish around its soft, slick sides and it wriggled mightily. He tightened his grip and the fish let out a croak. Bringing the fish up to eye level, Allen carefully looked at it. Finally, Allen started bending the hook out of the fish's mouth. The woman watched him remove the hook. "You know how to clean 'em?"

"I'm not keepin' him." Allen held the fish over the water to let it go.

"Wait," the woman screamed as she jumped up and ran toward him. "You're not gonna keep him?"

"No ma'am. I just wanted to catch one." Allen started to loosen his grip on the fish.

"Well, I'll take 'im." The woman looked incredulously at Allen as she snatched the fish out of his hand. "You come by the store, and I'll give you somethin' in trade, okay?" Allen's eyes opened wide as he remembered the woman from the Okra Cash and Carry.

"I remember now. You helped me get home one night when I was lost. You can have the fish. You helped me then; now I'll help you. How's that?"

"Well, that's right neighborly of you, son. You say I helped you get home?" She trotted over to her bucket, took out a metal stringer and started attaching the fish to it.

"Yeah, I mean, yes ma'am. It was a long time ago. I was lost and you gave me directions on how to get home."

"Is that right? I guess I've given out a couple hundred sets of directions in my day. It's kinda nice to see someone who remembers a good deed." She threw the strung up fish into the river and attached the other end of the string to a stick along the bank. "You know you look a might familiar to me, too. But I couldn't really say. But I'll tell you what—a young fella like you who remembers folks and returns a favor is awful nice to see. Most young'uns nowadays think you gotta have some sorta big plan for things to work out, and they all gotta start at the top. For some reason kids think you walk out and there's some wonderful life just waiting for you."

"Yeah," Allen shifted his weight from one foot and then the other. "Kids sure are silly, huh?"

The woman looked sideways at him. "Uh huh. And they think they gotta get this and get that and they wanna have more and more stuff, but it ain't stuff, is it?"

Allen nodded blankly, remembering Joey's and Jimbo's good fortune and his own jealousy over it. "Nah, I mean no ma'am. It's not about stuff." But Allen didn't buy it much.

The woman was threading another long worm on her hook and she paused long enough to toss one to Allen, who started threading it on like he had just seen the woman thread hers on. The woman tried not to watch Allen, but she glanced over at the last second and saw he had, in fact, done a nice job of it. "You know, son, it's good to see a fella like you who can just be what he wants to be. You wanna be happy, just be happy. It ain't a big secret. Like the man said, most folks are about as happy as they wanna be. And you wanna be a good person, you just be a good person, right? Everybody knows what's good. Folks all over got pretty much the same notion of what's good. All a person's gotta do is realize what he already knows and see he's gotta choice. If'n he chooses to be good, then whatta you know, he's good." Allen nodded again, but the woman wasn't talking to him so much as she was talking out her thoughts.

"But you know, even if you know what's right and decide to do what's right, there comes a time when you have to see that there's more, something a lot more that comes from somewhere deep inside o' you and then you gotta choose all over ag'in, only this time it's harder 'cause there ain't no reason to choose to follow what's inside o' you. You can't see it and it ain't even always real logical-like but you just up and decide one day that you believe in something what there ain't no good reason for and suddenly everything is differ'nt." She gave a little start, as if she suddenly realized that she wasn't speaking to the young man anymore and now tried to redirect her conversation. "You understand what I'm talking about, son?"

"Well, actually, I guess I do a bit." Allen was feeling the slow pull of the current on the tackle as it settled into the river. "So you're saying that if a person wants to be rich and famous, he's making a big mistake." Allen felt a tug on the line and pulled back on his fishing pole which was jerking and dancing with life on the other end of the line.

"No, it ain't a mistake, exactly. It's a person's right to choose. What I might decide idn't what everybody oughta decide. All I'm sayin' is that at some point, even if'n you decide to try to be rich and famous, you'll come to a point where you're gonna have to decide all over ag'in." She looked over and saw Allen fighting the fish. She reeled her line in disgustedly, under the pretense of checking her bait. Allen's pole was nearly doubled by the weight of the fish. He walked the fish up onto the gravel. The fish flopped on the ground and Allen reached over and picked it up.

"You want this one, too?" Allen had to hold it with two hands to keep from dropping it.

"Yeah, sure, why not? But you gotta come by the store an' let me pay you back. It wouldn't be right otherwise."

"Okay, but tell me, are you some kinda preacher or something? When I was at the store before, all those years ago, you said some stuff about faith and everything."

"Preacher?" She laughed and swung the stringer back into the river where it landed with a huge splash. "Naw, I ain't a preacher. I got beliefs though. Ev'rybody's got beliefs, right? Maybe I just share mine too much. Or maybe other folks don't share theirs enough. Seems to me we oughta talk about things that are important." Allen didn't answer but considered what the woman had said. He had rethreaded the tattered remains of the worm on his hook and now he swung the pole, the sinker pulling the line from his pole in a high-pitched whine. The current picked up the weight and slowly pulled the hook into the channel. The woman had thrown her tackle back out as well and now she went back to her monologue.

"Yeah, if'n folks don't talk, how they ever gonna find out about each other. Seems to me folks has a natural tendency towards sociableness, you know, like it's in their nature to be around other folks and in'eract." Allen's head started to hurt as he tried to figure out where she might go with this train of thought. He felt a strong pull on the line and yanked back sharply on his pole, setting the hook deep into the fish's mouth. When he pulled back, he slipped on the rocks and the woman stopped talking to look over. She reeled in her line rapidly. "Aw, hell. You gotta 'nother one? Damnations, boy, you're puttin' on my nerves somethin' fierce." She started gathering her equipment and mumbling to herself. "Anything I cain't stand it's some smart alecky kid catchin' all the damn fish and gloatin' over you 'bout it. Me, I'm fishin' out here forty years and this here damn punk comes in an' starts to . . ." She trailed off her thought as she picked up her tackle.

"You want this one, too?" Allen hoped to soothe her anger.

"Hell no, boy. What'sa matter with you. Why, you can take that fish and shove it, for all I care." Her chest puffed with anger and pride.

Allen pulled the fish up on the rocks. "What'd I do? You're the one who gave me the bait and all. I wasn't trying to do anything." His voice was plaintive and tired. The woman seemed to get more agitated the more Allen spoke. It didn't make any sense to apologize, of course, but Allen couldn't figure anything else to say. "I'm sorry, really."

"Yes, so I see!" She yelled as she stomped up the bank. Suddenly Allen felt like a teenager again, and not in a way he liked. He felt like a child who couldn't do anything right. He wanted to try to make it up to the woman although it wasn't his fault he had caught fish.

"You sure you don't want this fish?" He called after her, holding up the grey five-pounder.

"Look, kid. I don't want your damn fish and I don't want to hear any more of your pinko philosophy either, you hear?"

"Pinko philosophy? I didn't say anything about philosophy. You're the one who was going on like some hillbilly existential pragmatist." The woman turned at the top of the bank and glared back at Allen.

"Hillbilly! Existentialist! Oh, yeah that's the way to talk to an old woman. Call me names. Cut me to the quick. It's all right. I probably don't have many years left anyway. You're just like my boy Jimbo. He's alla time sassin' me too and belittlin' my beliefs and it'll kill me sure one day." She waved her free hand and looked to the heavens.

"Jimbo?" Allen dropped the fish on the gravel and it squirmed back toward the water.

"Yeah, that's my boy." She said it prouder now.

"Jimbo?" The fish flopped towards the water.

"Yeah, my boy's name is Jimbo." She said peevishly.

"Jimbo who owns the car lot now? That Jimbo?" The fish made the edge of the river, found his bearings, and slithered off with a splash.

"Yeah, that's him." She was proud again. "You've prolly seen him on the TV, aincha?" Allen nodded, his mouth hanging open. "He's done right well for hisself. He give some money to the community college and they've asked him to speak at the graduation next week." Allen felt his head getting hot. The old woman nodded at him as she turned to walk over the hill. "They're gonna make him an honorary doctor o' philosophy at the same time." And she disappeared over the hill. Allen felt his head spinning, and the horizon tilted as he felt the air leave his lungs. He looked down and saw the brown pebbles racing up to greet his face just before everything went black.

Objective Notion

There is no opinion so absurd but that some philosopher will express it.
                                                                    -Cicero

When Allen came to, his head still whirled with confusion. Allen tried to piece things together, gathering his tackle and thoughts. It seemed that everywhere he looked Jimbo the Moron, the Idiot, the Redheaded Sumo Wrestler, The Thing, the Hand Crusher, was standing there, mocking him. Allen couldn't believe it. Here sat Allen Johnson, a reasonably intelligent, reasonably well-educated, reasonably handsome fellow driving a fifteen-year-old Pinto, trying to figure out what to do with his life, wondering what sort of work to do, waiting desperately for that moment that would send him out of the bonds of obscurity and moderate poverty and into the limelight of the world. On the other hand, an illiterate, antisocial lummox who lived in a garage receives an honorary doctoral degree, builds a thriving business, has a chauffeur driven Lincoln, and ends up on television for everyone to view his resplendent success. There was no odd-shaped jar or box that Allen would fit in.

Allen, lost in thought, barely remembered driving to his parents' house. When he walked in the door of the house, in the living room was his mother dusting the plastic cover on the lamp shade, humming softly with a slight smile on her face. She looked up excitedly as Allen scuffled in the room. "Oh, honey, you're back. Carla called. She and John Wesley are coming down in the morning. Isn't that wonderful?" She bent over to pick up a tiny piece of lint on the sofa.

Allen watched her inspect the thready culprit. "Mom, why do you worry over this room so much? No one ever comes in here. You won't even allow us in here."

"It's for company." She needlessly ran the cloth over an already polished end table.

Allen raised his eyebrows. "Mom, you don't allow company in here."

She turned and looked benignly at Allen, a grimy young man with just a speck of dried blood on a corner of his ear. "That's not true, honey. Your father and I always entertain in here."

"Well, when my friends came over they weren't allowed in here."

"Oh Allen, you're so silly. Your friends weren't company." She turned and dusted a picture frame that held a primitive oil painting of the Johnsons done when the four of them had visited New Orleans for a week. Allen, fifteen at the time, thought it was the best vacation the family had ever taken. He had stopped and peered in every door on Bourbon Street. One barker had even tried to get Allen in the door, but his father had yanked him back onto the sidewalk. His mother acted as if Allen wasn't leering at every prostitute along the street, commenting that New Orleans was a "disgusting place" and that "there wasn't a good Christian within a hundred miles of the place." Allen decided that should probably be in the brochures, but he kept that opinion to himself.

Remembering the trip, Allen considered taking Carla and John Wesley there but decided against it. "So Carla and John Wesley will be here tomorrow. That is good. I've got some big news for them."

Mrs. Johnson turned quickly around again. "Big news? What is it Allen? Are you going back to the bank?" She loved news about her family she could share with Carol.

Allen clenched his teeth and snarled at his mother. "I could not possibly go back to some place I have never been, Mother."

His mother stood blankly in front of Allen, watching the vein in his forehead throb. "What in the world are you talking about, Allen?"

"Mother, I have never worked in a bank. I have, however, worked at a savings and loan center." He said as if he were speaking to a kindergartner. "A bank and a savings and loan center are two very different things."

"Oh, fiddle-faddle," his mother waved at him. "Are you going back to that wonderful job you had or not?"

"I am not going back, Mother." Allen calmed himself deliberately. "I have decided that one should never go back. Our lives are like bicycles. We must maintain our direction and keep going ever forward, or else we will tumble as surely as a bicycle with no impetus." He waved solemnly and looked far away.

"You're making no sense whatsoever, Allen, and you're starting to rant and rave like a madman. Carla and I decided that what was wrong with you is that—"

"What is 'wrong' with me, Mother?" Allen tried to maintain the pose he had assumed when he was pontificating, but he could feel his face reddening. "'What is wrong with me?' Why, Mother dearest, there is absolutely nothing wrong with me. And I certainly don't want to hear about your discussions in that vein. You are allowed your opinions, of course, as is everyone, but do not be misled." He wagged his finger at his mother who stood silently still in front of her son, wondering who in the world he was. He was still in his pose and now it started to feel awkward, so he changed his stance slightly, making him look as if he was walking an invisible tightrope. "No, Mother. You should not mistake the Jacksonian notion that every poor slob is entitled to an opinion to mean that one opinion is as good as another. In fact, we should change the expression. Instead of saying, 'To each his own,' we should say, 'Each blithering idiot is allowed his own opinion, no matter how absurd and ill-founded it may be.'"

"I don't have time for this, Allen. I have work to do."

Allen dropped his pose now that his mother had turned around and started dusting again.

"I have too much to do to listen to you go on about all this nonsense about opinions," she continued.

"Too much to do? What, cleaning an already clean house?"

"Now Allen, you know cleanliness is next to Godliness."

"You're right, Mother." Allen dropped it, turned and retreated towards the kitchen. He found the paper that he never finished reading from that morning because of his dramatic exit. On the front page was a picture of Reverend Pondermust and a group of other staid men, shovels in hand, preparing to break ground on the new city youth entertainment center. Reverend Pondermust described the new center in the interview as, "A place for the teens of Evanston to experience the joy of youth without the distractions and bad influences of television, or loud rock music, or dancing, or those terrible video games rotting the minds of today's youth." What in the world kids would be allowed to do in the teen center had not yet been determined, but it was guaranteed to be "fun and wholesome." Conveniently located next to the teen center just happened to be the good preacher's own church.

Allen shook his head at the picture. "Well, at least you know your agenda, Rev," he said to the picture. He turned the page and a glamour photo of his former partner in dance and study and whatever smiled back at him advertising some kind of insurance. Allen sighed at the picture of all those brown curls piled ever higher on her head. "Sharon Mellon

Insurance Agency," the ad read. "The Largest Insurance Agency in West Central Kentucky." Allen shook his head again. "And you, Sharon," he said out loud again, "showing me up and doing great. Why is everyone else doing great and I'm doing so badly?"

"Who are you talking to, Allen? Is someone here?" Allen's mother called from the next room. "Don't come into the living room."

Allen folded up the paper and left quietly through the back door. He wondered how long it would be before his mother would know that he had left. He also wondered where his father had gone. It was past time for him to be home from work. And Allen wondered why everyone he knew seemed to be a big success while he was not, despite the obvious disadvantages these other people had. His friends and acquaintances were visible, well-adjusted stalwarts of the community, yet to Allen, the deficiencies they each had outnumbered all of his—by his account. Not that Allen was necessarily a wonder child or anything, but even so he had some obvious advantages over them.

Allen walked aimlessly down the street, the same street where he and Joey had played chicken on their trusty Stingray bikes (often ending with skinned knees), where he had first garnered the attention of Red Schoendienst, and where he had fallen hopelessly in love with Karen Dobroski. It seemed like a different street then, and for that matter, a different Allen Johnson. In some ways, he knew what he wanted and how to go after it better then. He would be a famous baseball player and everyone would know his name. His daydreams then were so clear. But his daydreams now were different. Perhaps that was the answer. Maybe he needed to look at how his dreams had changed and then redirect his ideas accordingly. That was it! It was a new plan. A plan to overcome this ever deepening chasm of invisibility Allen was sinking into and the frustration that caused him. Maybe he could engage in a deep analysis of his daydreams, his reveries that he took great pride in, for Allen had practiced this skill very deliberately over the years. Daydreaming: the one skill that Allen felt he was most accomplished in.

Now that he thought about it, Allen had believed for a long time that there was a hidden value in daydreams. He had decided when he was in college that society had largely discounted the inherent value of daydreams through a pathological preoccupation with production as opposed to reproduction. Allen saw daydreams as a mythic recapturing, a reproducing of the primitive connection between the psyche and the world. After all, reveries brought people relaxation and, since people control the outcome, guaranteed success, something greatly valuable (even if it's only fantastical). And then there was the benefit that daydreams bring out folks' creative side. Surely Allen did not need to justify creativity, but if he did, then creativity could be justified on the grounds that folks imagining results of various options better equip them to make better choices. He felt like maybe he was on to some track here, but he couldn't tell where it was going yet. His train of thought was heading in its own direction. Allen ambled slowly on, aimlessly, caught up in his analysis.

Now that he thought about it, Allen had noticed that the content of his daydreams had changed subtly over the years, particularly as he approached and passed that magical, mysterious age of thirty (oh, those birthdays with zeroes). Through his analysis, he found that the goals, the life dreams that he had held so dear and so confidently in his younger days, had been left unfulfilled and abandoned as life unfolded. A sense of loss and melancholy and a bit of frustration accompanied this discovery. Life would not allow Allen Johnson to pass without making a shambles of at least some of his dreams. In a life that has so many different variables—families, economics, fortune, and misfortune—it was inevitable, he supposed. In fact, now that he thought about it, the loss of some of those life dreams had made possible the realization of others and had made room for the formulation of others still.

Allen picked up a stick from the sidewalk, tapping it on the ground as he walked. As he passed a pair of garbage cans, he rapped a quick drum roll on the top of one.

Allen paused for a moment to regain his train of thought. He turned down Parrish Avenue. Where was he? He had noticed that his daydreams had changed. Yeah, that was it. His daydreams had changed subtly over the years. Always just a bit athletically inclined, many of those reveries of his twenties, or even younger, had him drawing the crowds to witness in awe his incredible skills, crossing that boundary from a weekend sports enthusiast to become a real athlete (he recalled briefly that baseball would never be the same, and he had to chuckle at the pleasure that daydream had brought him). But now, as he engaged in the same type of reverie, he was not using his physical skills, but his intellectual skills, as he wrote philosophical treatises and answered the questions posed by humans since time began. As his own reality had changed, his fantasies had changed.

But when he considered it, it was to be expected after all, since part of the appeal of a daydream to Allen was that on some minute level, there was something marginally possible about the dream. He would not dream that he was in some way super human (at least not since he had given up the conspiracy theory), since it could hold no glimmer of occurring. Of course Allen knew he would not really be able to resolve all the philosophical issues before humanity, but certainly that was more likely than his receiving a professional contract to play sports at thirty after working behind a desk for all these years. And if it was more likely, then there must have been some infinitesimal chance it could occur. There was a tiny piece of actuality attached to the dream. It had, in a sense, matter, concreteness, substance.

The light was fading now, and Allen stumbled on a crack in the sidewalk. He caught himself but allowed the momentum to take him to a sitting position on the step of the house he was in front of. In fact, Allen decided that if anyone had seen it, he or she might believe he intentionally sat down, perhaps a little roughly, but intentionally nonetheless.

This comforted him, and Allen returned to his thoughts. But what about those other dreams, the life dreams that he saw as goals, as real possibilities requiring his attention and his concerted effort, the dreams he was now trying to get a handle on? Were these dreams not affected by the subtle change in his daydreams? Allen decided they must be, since if the realization of actuality can affect the fantasy, the reverie was irrevocably connected to reality. Perhaps in his train of thought he was making too much of the connection, but Allen decided if a person learns (at least partially) to imagine by engaging in daydreams, then if the terms of those daydreams had changed, the images had changed. And if those images changed, wouldn't that effect the other images of his life and his life dreams? Allen's head began to ache, but he didn't want to lose this chain. He concentrated fiercely. This change in life dreams wouldn't only be the change that was necessitated by realizing the difference between possibility and probability.

Of course, as Allen had matured, there were times (like when the dream to strike out twenty-seven batters in one baseball game lost its appeal due to its improbability) he had had to lower his sights to try to realize dreams that might actually have a chance of occurring. But he should not try to minimize the importance of that change, he decided. Something was lost and something was gained by all these changes. When he decided to lower his scope for what was more likely, he lost the opportunity to see himself as achieving the level of greatness that he might have strived for originally. On the other hand, he gained the sense of accomplishment that accompanies realized dreams. So he was faced with a dilemma. If he lowered his expectations, he became accomplished at mediocrity. If he kept his goals high, he became a frustrated egoist. Surely there was some middle ground. Allen closed his eyes and thought very hard. He was close to the end of something. He must continue. With his eyes closed, the world seemed much calmer and Allen felt a sense of relaxation come over him as he wound his way through these ideas.

Accomplishment, of course! It was the difference between the dreams of his everyday life and his life of reverie. His life dreams—often forced into a mold both confining and possible—were so frequently same and uninspired, like a nest within which he pushed the rough edges out (comforting in its way). His daydreams, however, were conquering and glorious and always fulfilling. And since they had that tiny glimmer of possibility, however tenuous, they had a speck of actuality that brought Allen emotional and psychological gain. When he let himself go in his fantasies, he allowed his mind to wander aimlessly. When he did that, he provided himself with a freedom. That freedom centered on the matter, the substance that he took and built the dream upon and that kept him from dwelling in mediocrity. The thoughts came more readily now, and Allen let them flow through his head and soothe him.

What's more, the benefit of these reveries was not mere escape, Allen realized. It was more than vicarious living where Allen could take refuge from the depressing humdrum of his otherwise sometimes bleak life. By means of daydreams, perhaps he could keep from having a bleak life, for the substance of the daydream was the same substance of the life dreams. In fact, that substance of the life dreams might even be the result of his daydreams as well as the source of new ones. In this way, daydreams could inform Allen's life dreams, and, by keeping the fantastic in touch with the actual, provide him with the spark of unreality that was necessary for his life to contain an edge of excitement even when his daily schedule seemed overwhelming. Allen felt relieved and relaxed as the thoughts started to come to their conclusion.

So there it was. Allen needed his daydream to relax, to gain in an otherwise ungainly world, and to inform the new life goals he formulated along his way. Dreaming was just as important to Allen's success as meticulous planning was. If he had no goal, where was the purpose of the plan? Each day, as Allen had waited in traffic, switching lanes in the vain attempt to gain a minute of stress, or as he had sorted through endless mounds of meaningless junk mail that would find its way to his desk (when he had been employed), he had needed to take the time to let his mind engage a reverie. He had dreamed of successes. He had won. And if the boss (when he had a boss) had asked him why he was late for work, he should have replied (if he had had the idea then or the nerve) with a wonderful riddle that he had been working all the way to the office (he wished now that he had been so brazen with his supervisors). The train of thought stopped. Allen had thought it all the way through. Allen sighed a deep sigh of completion and fatigue, leaned against the post that held the mailbox that said Dobroski on it, and fell into a deep sleep.

Evolution

Man is the only animal that laughs and weeps; for he is the only animal that is struck with the difference between what things are, and what they ought to be.
                                                                              -William Hazlitt

"What are you doing out here?" The voice was soft and fearful. Allen awoke with a start, jolting upright. The owner of the soft, scared voice jumped backwards. "Don't hurt me, please."

"Huh?" Allen rubbed the sleep from his eyes.

"Are you one of those homeless people, out of work and desperate and all that?" The voice spoke from behind its place of refuge.

"Huh? Oh, well, maybe, when you put it that way. Where am I?" Allen looked about him, and at just about the same time that he remembered where he was, his eyes focused on the shadowy blond hair that still had a ribbon in it. As he recognized the still pretty face of Karen, his childhood dream, made younger by the faint glow of the street lamp a half block away, he let out a slow, sad moan.

"Are you okay? Tell me something; will you work for food? Or is that really just a trick like everybody says? Wait a minute. What are you doing?" Allen struggled to stand. The soft voice escalated almost an octave, "Don't hurt me! It was just a question. You don't have to answer. Don't kill me, please." Allen's joints were stiff in the cool night air and he teetered as he stood. Karen jumped back again. "Please don't kill me. I was just going to give you some food. Here." She rolled a can of jack mackerel that looked as if it had been in the pantry a decade down the sidewalk and it bumped his foot as he stood. Allen was loosening up a little now. He reached down and picked up the can.

"Jack mackerel? Is this the best you could do, Karen? This can is older than I am. Thanks, but I'd prefer a steak and a baked potato."

"Do I know you? How did you know my name? Who are you? Never mind; you don't have to answer. Don't hurt me." She became very defensive and even more frightened. She backed away slowly.

"Don't worry, Karen. I won't hurt you. I'm not a mugger and most of the time I'm not a street person, although I did grow up on this street, just down around the corner on the next block. Not that I think you ever noticed."

"Richard? Richard Sauers, is that really you?"

Allen's chin dropped and he looked at Karen in disbelief. "No. No, I'm not Richard Sauers. Jeez! Can it really be that all those years that we lived in the same neighborhood and went to the same schools and even graduated together that you never, ever saw me? I can't believe it! I'm Allen Johnson. From the Class of '76?" Karen nodded blankly. She was utterly stumped. "Well, I might have known. It was worse than I thought. Back then I tried everything in my power to get you to notice me, and now I discover that I failed far more completely than I could ever have imagined." Allen sat down again suddenly and heavily and put his head in his hands.

"I'm sorry, Albert. I guess I really should remember you, but there were so many boys and there was cheerleading and pom-pom squad and pep club, and you know. I was just so busy all the time. I feel awful, really. And now, to find out that by not noticing you, I turned you into a street person, it's just too awful." She broke into deep sobs. "Why does everything always come back to my fault? If only I had said something nice to you once, maybe you could have made something of yourself. You could have been a banker or something." She sat down next to Allen now and buried her eyes in her hands and snuffled inconsolably.

"Huh?" Allen looked up at her sharply. "Why did you say that? Why did you say I could have been a banker?"

"Well, it just seemed like something a poor, depressed, street person might want to be." She shrugged and sniffled.

"I'm not a street person, Karen. I just fell asleep is all. I'm visiting my parents and I went for walk and got lost in my thoughts and next thing I know you're rolling me a can of decayed jack mackerel."

Karen's tears stopped suddenly. "You're not homeless?"

"No." Allen shook his head.

"You're not hungry?" Her eyebrows rose.

"Not for this." Allen held up the can.

Karen snatched the can from him. "Well, then give it back, Alvin. If you don't want it, someone else will." She flipped her hair around swatting Allen in the face with it. He was overwhelmed by the scent of perfume in her hair.

"Allen." His name managed to tumble out of his mouth.

"What?" She flipped her hair again and looked at Allen, her eyes glistening with moisture in the light of the street lamp.

"My name is Allen, not Albert, not Alvin, not Richard. Allen. Allen Johnson. I lived all my school years at thirteen eleven Saint Ann Street, just around the corner. I know you don't remember me, but try to get my name right, please?" Allen's thoughts raced back to his youth.

"Well, aren't we awfully high and mighty for a street person?" Karen wagged her head in contempt. When she did, the waves of perfume wafted over Allen again. He felt a little light headed. He blinked slowly. Where was he?

"I'm not a street person, Karen," he said weakly.

Karen saw him blinking back his confusion. "Then what do you do?"

"Well, actually, I'm between positions." Allen breathed deeply the inebriating, perfumed air of his childhood fantasy.

Karen nodded knowingly. "That's what I thought you'd say. You're embarrassed. I understand." She leaned closer to him. "You know, maybe I should mentor you. I'm a 'people-person,' you know. I can help you. Then I can make up for turning you into a homeless man. What is it you've always dreamed of doing, Al?" Allen's eyes blurred as he sat next to Karen Dobroski. How many fantasies?

"Karen, I just quit my job at a bank so I can go get my doctorate in philosophy." He sighed. Karen's eyes widened.

"Why? Why would you want a degree in philosophy? That doesn't make sense."

"Karen, I already have a degree in philosophy." His voice had a hint of irritation in it.

"Of course you do, Arvin." She patted his knee paternally, which sent a thrill up Allen's leg. "And where did you get this 'degree in philosophy'?" She made quotation marks with her fingers.

"At the same university you went to, Karen." Allen reveled in Karen's touch.

"I see. Funny. I don't remember seeing you there." She said it as if she had caught him in a lie. She rested her hand on his knee now, finished with the patronizing pat.

"I know you didn't, Karen. That's hardly surprising." Allen felt the world spin. Allen wasn't sure, but this might actually have been one of the daydreams he sometimes engaged in when he had imagined he and Karen were passionate lovers in his youth and he tried very deliberately to go blind. Was this the night?

"I know!" Karen clapped her hands once enthusiastically. "Let's do some roleplaying. What do you think, Al? Want to do some roleplaying?" Allen saw his adolescent images of Karen in the teachers' lounge. She lowered her face so she could meet his eyes with hers, which were filled with concern.

"I don't know. I just . . ." Allen struggled to get out of his pubescent fugue. What was happening here?

"What is it you really want, Al?" Karen reached over and grabbed Allen's hands in support. "If you weren't living on the streets, where would you dream of sleeping tonight?"

"I'm not a street person, Karen." Allen turned slightly to face her. "And I have always dreamed of sleeping with . . ."

"Why, of course you aren't a street person, Al. Why, you're a fine, upstanding member of our little town. With a doctorate in philosophy!" Karen gave him a practiced, sincere smile, but Allen was still blinking from the perfume, the touch, and his own reverie and missed it.

"Allen. Allen Johnson." Allen's head was beginning to spin. Where was he, exactly? "And I don't have a doctorate. I do have a bachelor's, however."

"Whatever. We can do this together. You'll see." Karen leaned toward Allen and allowed her shoulder to lean against his as she looked at her wrist watch in the dark. She could not have read the time, but Allen was becoming oblivious. "Oh, it's so late. I can't believe we're sitting out here talking after so many years, Al. Just think of it. What if I hadn't come home this weekend to see my folks?" She shivered and sidled a tiny bit closer to Allen, as if for warmth. If it was cool, Allen did not feel it. Karen looked up into Allen's eyes and blinked once, slowly, earnestly. "I think I was meant to find you here tonight, Al."

"No, not Al; Allen. My name is Allen Johnson." It was as if saying his name would keep him sane. Karen was quiet, huddled close to Allen for warmth. This was definitely one of his adolescent dreams. The scent of her hair and her casual contact now was overpowering and Allen suddenly realized that he was rediscovering his own sexuality again, and the fact of that discovery was beginning to press uncomfortably against his jeans as he sat there huddled on the step next to his unrequited juvenile love. He wanted desperately to adjust himself but could think of no way to do so without being terribly obvious and embarrassing himself and Karen. Instead, Allen sat and suffered.

But the discomfort brought Allen to his senses and he remembered where he was and who he was (and, more importantly, who Carla was).

He took Karen's hand in his own and turned so that he was fully facing her. "Karen," Allen said gently and calmly, although he was still in considerable discomfort, "I really am very flattered by your attention, but it just wouldn't be right to get involved with you in any way. There was a time I would have killed to be where I am at this moment, but that was a different time and, well, a different dream. My dreams have changed and my life has changed and I cannot sit here on this step with you driving me nuts and pretend that isn't so."

"What?" Karen looked at him in confusion. "Are you saying you don't want my help to realize your dreams, Allen?" She pulled back now defensively. "I mean, surely my help is better than a soup kitchen." She said it as if it were a question.

"Oh no, Karen. You are very kind, and very generous. I mean, jack mackerel!" Allen squirmed a little to try to relieve the pressure in his pants.

"It's what we had. Sorry, Mr. Particular Hobo!" Karen stood suddenly, her indignation pouring from her. Allen stood up suddenly now to apologize or explain or something and almost doubled over with pain caused by his sudden movement. Karen smirked as she stared at Allen's jeans and he turned away from her and tried to make himself less obvious. It was too late to pretend she had not excited him, but he at least could make himself less conspicuous. "Well, it looks like at least some of you would like my company, Allen." She sneered slightly.

"Karen," Allen stood a little sideways to hide himself in the darkness, "you are very kind, but you and I just weren't meant to happen together. I thank you for your attention, and I am indeed quite flattered, but now I must go home." Allen hobbled sideways past Karen, who stood looking completely baffled.

When Allen finally reached the corner of Saint Ann Street, Karen turned up to go back into her house. She looked in her hand and saw that she was still holding the can of mackerel and she turned and threw the can as hard as she could down the street that Allen had just vacated. She clenched her fists and said softly into the cool May morning that was just beginning to lighten, "Someday, Allen Johnson, you will beg me for my help. You will find I don't give up on people so easily. I will save you from the streets of Evanston." Karen turned again and went into the house.

Meanwhile, Allen walked to his home in a strange mood. On the one hand, there was a certain frustration in not fulfilling his adolescent dream with Karen. At least he thought that was what was going on. On the other hand, he believed he had done the right thing, and knowing that, he felt good about himself. He felt, for a change, that he was in control of at least some parts of his life (if not his body). He wished that he could tell Carla what a good thing he had done, but then he realized that he would have to explain to her why the enticement was so strong and perhaps even about the nature of his adolescent fantasies with Karen and perhaps even the extent of his attraction this evening to her. No, it was better not to even bring it up.

When he walked up to his parents' home, it was completely dark in the early morning grey except for a light on in the kitchen. Allen walked around the house and peered in the kitchen window. His father was sitting at the table, drinking a cup of coffee and reading the morning paper. Allen went in the back door.

"Hi, Dad." Allen couldn't figure how to explain the lateness of the hour. His father did not put down the paper.

"Good morning, son. Would you like some coffee?" His father looked up briefly, then went on scanning the headlines. Could it be he wasn't even going to ask? Allen retrieved the cup with the web of cracks.

Allen poured the coffee, and the gurgle of the liquid was stark in the quiet kitchen. Allen sat opposite his father. "Can I see the sports?"

"Sure." His father handed him the paper. The silence was overwhelming.

Allen pretended to read the paper, but he couldn't concentrate. Finally he couldn't stand it anymore. He put the paper down and put his head in his hands. "Okay, okay, I'm sorry I was out all night. You don't have to badger me about it!"

His father was stoic. "I don't remember asking you a thing, other than if you wanted a cup of coffee." If Allen had closed his eyes, he could have believed it was Fred MacMurray in *My Three Sons*. His voice was calm and practiced. It was as if nothing could faze him.

"I went out for a walk to think and I fell asleep leaning up against a mailbox. Okay?"

"Uh huh. Sounds comfortable." His father took a sip of coffee. He was still focused on the front page.

"Well, not really," Allen sighed. "To tell you the truth, it was kinda strange. I ran into an old high school friend while I was out."

"Karen Dobroski?" His father interjected. Allen looked up sharply, telling his father he was correct. "I saw you asleep against Charlie's mailbox."

"You saw me?" Allen's chin dropped.

"Yeah. When you didn't come back for dinner I went out and saw you leaning against the post." He shrugged and sipped some more coffee. "I figured you'd come home when you were ready."

"You saw me sleeping on Karen Dobroski's doorstep and you didn't wake me?" Allen's eyes were wide.

"Nope." He continued to look at the paper. His patient posture was beginning to bug Allen.

"You know, Dad, when I was a kid, I had a terrible crush on Karen." Allen's face grew hot.

"Yeah, I know. Are you over it?" His father asked nonchalantly.

Allen looked up at his father, who only now looked over his paper at his son. "Yeah. Yeah, I am. But I didn't know that until tonight. You know something, Pop? You're a cagy old bird. I'm just beginning to see how you operate."

"I didn't do anything. Whatever happened, you did it." His father flipped the paper back over his eyes.

"Yeah, but you let me. You knew I had to do it myself, didn't you?" Allen stared at his father with mild confusion and respect.

"I had faith in you, Allen." He folded the section he was reading. "You done with the sports page yet?"

"Yeah, go ahead." Allen pushed the paper back over to his father. "That was a long time ago when I was so nuts about her. It's funny, really. I guess I've been over that crush for a long time and I just never stopped to think about it."

"Is that all you stopped to think about?" Mr. Johnson was peering at the baseball line scores.

Allen rose from the table. "No, Pop. I realized a bunch of stuff tonight. But I'm not ready to talk about it yet. I need to talk to Carla first."

"I understand, Allen. You want one of my world famous three egg omelets?" Allen's father rose from the table and pulled his robe around him.

"Yeah, I am pretty hungry," Allen made a face, "and I sure don't want any jack mackerel."

"Jack mackerel?" His father stopped and turned with a befuddled facial expression, "In an omelet?"

"It's a long story, Pop. I'll have to tell you about it someday. What can I do?" Allen stood up from the table.

"You chop up an onion. I'll get the cheeses out." And the two men set to work together.

Revolution

The farther one pursues knowledge, the less one knows.

-Lao-Tzu

When Carla arrived later that morning, there had been a few moments of mixed tenderness and tenseness. Relief, regret, and excitement all at once flooded Allen as he hugged his son and his wife-with-child. Though it had been only a few days since he had seen them (it had seemed like much longer), he was happy to see his family. So much had happened, and Allen had spent so much time thinking. He wanted to talk to Carla about his thoughts, about how, in a sense, he felt trapped by having a family despite the fact that he loved them all dearly. He would have to tell Carla at some time how he felt. It was too important for Allen not to tell her, especially after all she had put up with being married to him. But when they first arrived, Allen knew it just wasn't the right time.

That morning, Allen suddenly realized that he really did love Carla in a deeper and more profound way than he had ever thought of the word. Perhaps that was why he had felt so nebulous about the concept of "being in love." In fact, he had been working under a false notion of what love was and, consequently, had been unable to grasp the idea. Being in love wasn't fawning and exotic travel and expensive, dark restaurants (though those things were certainly nice). Being in love, Allen realized, was working every day, and cleaning the house, and making babies, and paying bills, and eating frozen pizzas when you are too tired to cook, and doing all of it together as a team because you like working together and being together. It might be mundane, but it was the reality of it. It was like the daydreams; once the importance of actuality in dreams was finally understood, they not only became earthier, but they also became more satisfying. Love was like that too.

When Allen's mother and father had finished hugging and offering seats and drinks to Carla and John (in the kitchen, not the living room), Allen's father had suddenly stood up and suggested that he and Grandma and John Wesley all go out for ice cream. Mrs. Johnson had started to explain that they had ice cream, but her husband shooed her out the door before she had finished the sentence. Finally, Allen and Carla were alone.

At first the awkwardness made them silent, as if they were meeting for the first time on a blind date. But after a couple of moments, Carla started to speak.

"Wait," he said softly. Allen had reached across the kitchen table to her and placed his finger on her lips. He brought her face close and he thought for just a moment about telling her what a noble fellow he had been the previous evening, but instead he picked up her hands and led her into his mother's pristine living room and pressed her into the couch and kissed her movingly.

"Oh, Allen—" Carla started.

"Sshhh." Allen groped, unbuttoned, and unzipped as if he were a young boy who had never done such a thing. And there on his mother's immaculate couch he made love to his pregnant wife Carla and, at the same time, released twenty years of frustration over wasted fantasies. Carla ended up dizzy with the fury of Allen's passion. "Let me catch my breath. Maybe you should visit your folks more often, Allen." Carla sat limp in the couch as if she had been dropped from a high place.

After a moment, as they were hurriedly redressing in case Allen's parents and their son suddenly returned, Allen stopped and gave Carla a deep gaze and said very evenly, "Carla, I love you. I'm sorry for the pain I have caused you. But now, I have a plan. Let's take a walk. I've gotta tell you something."

"Walk? I don't think so, Stallion." Carla didn't move. Her blouse was still only partially buttoned but she was enervated.

"I'm serious, Carla." Allen stood and reached his hand out to his wife. "Come on, honey. Let's go. We need to talk."

"Oh, okay. But I'm going to remember this." She gave him a furtive glance.

"Carla, stop that." Allen smirked. "Come on." Allen pulled her up and she barely had time to finish putting herself together before he pulled her out the door. They walked down to the corner and turned past the trash cans and down Parrish Avenue, Allen practically dragging Carla along until they neared his resting spot the night before. Then he slowed his gait and Carla, still glowing from the passion, wrapped herself around Allen's arm, nuzzling up close to him.

"Mmmmm," she purred at him as she rubbed her cheek against his shoulder. "Let's go back and play some more, Allen." Allen hoped Karen was watching.

"Carla, I want to go back to school." He whispered in her ear.

"What?" Carla stopped now and scowled at Allen. "What do you want to study? Where would you go to school? What about getting a job? What will we do for money? We've got a baby coming. Did you forget that?"

"Whoa. Slow down, honey." Allen thought he saw the venetian blinds in Karen's living room separate and this brought a satisfied smile to Allen's face. Allen took Carla's arm in his and they started walking again. "Let's talk about it. All I said is, I want to go to school. I don't know if I can, but it's worth talking about. I have to tell you, this week has been very strange, but in some ways I feel like I've taken some control over my life, and I like that feeling. I don't want to give it up, if I can help it."

"Okay. That's fair enough." She nodded her head trying to be understanding. "What is it you want to study, first."

"Well," he sucked in a breath for confidence, "getting a master's in philosophy from the university is what I had in mind."

"Then what?" Carla's eyebrows furrowed. "Is a master's any more marketable than a bachelor's?"

"Well, probably not, really. But I want to try for it. It may be more for me than for anything else, just to prove to myself I can do it. Then, maybe I could go for a doctorate and then get a job teaching somewhere, maybe at a junior college or a little college perhaps." His hand on her arm had grown moist from nervousness as he spoke.

"Hmmm. You think you have the patience to teach, Allen? I really don't see you as the teaching type." Carla waddled next to him along Parrish Avenue.

"Maybe not," he said looking at the horizon, "but I think I want to try. And I have another idea, too. I'm working on an idea about how our dreams are related to our lives."

"Sounds like psychology to me." She also looked to the horizon but she couldn't see whatever it was that Allen was gazing at.

"Psychology, philosophy, different sides of the same coin. But I'm not talking about night dreams, I'm talking about daydreams."

"Ha!" Carla stopped walking and grinned. "Daydreams! You want to be some sort of daydream guru? You want to go back to school and move our family so you can become a professional daydreamer? My God, Allen. I believe you're going through a midlife crisis for sure. That's it! You're afraid of getting older, aren't you? That's what this all about. On your thirtieth birthday, you suddenly wake up and see that you have only so many more years left before I ship you off to a nursing home, and for some reason you think you have to do everything before that; so now you go and quit your job so you can become a professional goof-off."

"That's not fair, Carla." His eyes were no longer on the horizon but glued to the ground, "Maybe some of it is my age. I don't know. But think about it, honey. For once, I could have some control. I could do something that I want to do."

"You're a bit young for all this angst, aren't you, Allen?" She tugged his arm and they resumed a slow stroll. "Thirty really isn't midlife, you know."

"It's not a midlife crisis. Well, at least I don't think it is. If it is, it's your fault any way." This last part slipped out before Allen could stop himself.

"What? This is all my doing? How does that work, my soon-to-be middle-aged husband?" She blew off his remark and they walked towards Daviess Street.

"Middle aged? That's great. Middle aged at thirty." Allen snorted, "And you're just a baby of twenty-nine. That's okay. I can take it. After all, it wasn't like I haven't known it was coming. So now you think I'm middle aged." Trying to calm Allen down, Carla softened her voice.

"Well, it's the way you sound, Allen."

"In a way, maybe you're right. Maybe I am worried about getting older, about eventually becoming middle aged and never having done the things I always dreamed of doing. It sounds ridiculous, doesn't it? Middle aged. It has such a thudding sound. Middle aged sounds like Middle Ages, like serfs and peasants and men riding around in those clumsy metal suits chasing the notion of chivalry, with knowledge and learning and all that stuff placed lowly on the list of importance. Middle aged. I can't see myself being middle aged." Allen gave Carla a playful nudge. "But it is your fault, you know."

"Well, I wouldn't worry too much about it, Allen. You've got a couple of good years left before we have to shoot you." Carla smirked and leaned close to Allen as they crossed Daviess, moving farther and farther from the Johnsons' house. The day was warm and a cool breeze tossed Carla's bangs. Allen felt as close to Carla as he had since their college days, and he knew she would have to let him go back to college. "So back up here. How is it my fault, Mr. Daydreamer?"

Allen gazed into the sky and placed a finger on his chin, contemplating. "Well, I'm not sure, but I think maybe it all started with adolescence." Allen found himself impersonating Dr. Kamew. "Yesh, I think that'sh it." He glanced at Carla to see if she was getting his pose, but she was watching the sidewalk. Allen dropped the Kamew accent. "If I didn't want to be middle aged, my first big mistake was going through adolescence. That's when I put down my cars and trucks and put the imaginary horse in the make-believe barn and started on my unending quest for a girlfriend. It was the beginning of the end."

"It couldn't have been my fault, then." Carla looked up at Allen. "I didn't know you when you were an adolescent."

"That doesn't matter. See, I'm not saying the girls I knew were my downfall. I'm saying my quest for a girlfriend was, and eventually that means you. When a boy is thirteen and wants to get the attention of that certain little girl who stands at the corner, her books held close to her chest, flipping her long blonde, err, brown hair, he knows immediately a truth. Yes, that girl might say hello to him, she might even pass the time, but if he can drive, well, that's the ticket to real glory, right? He knows then that he must be sixteen. Then he can drive her around. They can go on real dates and then they can be a couple. They can sit at the Dairy Doodle and folks will say, 'Oh, there's Allen and Carla,' or whatever, and then he's got a girlfriend. And then that young man's life is complete. He has that flippy girl all to himself. And you were one of those girls on the corner flipping her hair and making the poor boys like me insane, weren't you?"

Carla laughed. "Maybe."

"Yeah, maybe. But then of course a problem crops up on the way to sixteen, doesn't it? All the other fellows grow up too, and suddenly, having a driver's license isn't such a novelty. What's a fellow to do? Well, if he were a college student, a big man on campus, then he would be bound to get Carla's attention." Allen rambled on.

"Maybe. That's all that attracted me to you, Mr. Philosophy," she nudged him playfully with her elbow, "but I still don't see that I'm to blame for your aging process."

"Poor Carla." Allen shook his head in mock sorrow. "I'm sorry; I don't really mean to blame you, but don't you see if you had only been my girlfriend back then, back when I was sixteen, or better yet, when I was thirteen, I might never be in this middle age predicament."

"Oh, I see." Carla's eyes twinkled with amusement, "I made you grow up and become a college student."

"Yeah, and you know what comes next. When I went to college, so did a hundred thousand, no, millions of other fellows. And then some went off and joined the military, but that's a whole different story. And then some others went ahead and got jobs, but I remember most of those guys already had girlfriends, except for Joey, and so most of them had no real reason to go to college. I suppose, in that sense, they were able to revel in a blissful arrested development." Allen was losing himself in his train of thought.

Carla looked up at Allen now and shook her head in disbelief. "Now let me see if I have this. The only reason to go to college is to get a girl? Allen, you're silly. You know that, don't you?"

Allen didn't answer; he had another train of thought going, and as he had discovered the night before, if he would just follow it through, he would feel a sense of completion, of accomplishment, even. He had enjoyed that feeling the night before and wanted to try to recapture it. "Yeah, but then going to college will only do for a while. If a guy didn't get a girl, he's really pressed for it now. Even if he got a girlfriend, he still has to worry about keeping her. Sure, even the weird fellows like me sometimes find a girl who doesn't follow the playbook in front of her and, therefore, doesn't know she can hold out for the bigger catch; but every girl eventually figures it out."

"Watch out, Allen. What is it you think a woman wants, anyway?" They turned down Lewis Street and headed up town. The cars tooled past blindly. Allen and Carla were equally oblivious to the passing cars.

Allen paused in his walk and shoved his hands into his back pockets. "Well, I don't know. The same thing a fellow wants, I guess. Security and companionship and a pretty face to look at and someone who adores them. That's why a fellow can't stop at college. He has to graduate from college and get a job. Oh, what a loathsome thing to do. Leaving college was tough." Allen shook his head and they continued their stroll.

"I don't know about that." Carla scoffed. "Seems to me college was hard work, at least some of the time."

"I disagree, Carla. I know when we were college students, we would have cried foul over it, but the fact of the matter is, a college is one of the most sublime spots on earth. Only when you are in college can you wallow in such questions as what constitutes the difference between knowledge and conceited opinion. And when you leave, you will never ask those questions again. In fact, at some point you will wonder why on earth anyone ever did ask such a question. But while you're in college, you can ask questions like that, and you can even keep a straight face while you do. But once you are out, that's it. No more academe, no more silly questions, no more fun and games. *You have graduated, and you must work.*"

"You make it sound so depressing." Carla held onto Allen's arm as she made her way with him towards downtown Evanston.

"It is depressing. That's what I'm saying. When I graduated from college, I had to work, and that's when I really began to age. I got up at six or seven and got ready for work very carefully so I could try to make an impression on some boss that I actually despised. And why? Because all those other hundreds of thousands of other fellows went off to college and were out there working too. Having a college degree didn't mean getting that fat pay check. No, as a college graduate, I found out I had to pay some dues and that meant long hours at lousy pay. If I worked hard enough and some muckety-muck noticed, then I might, I just might, get ahead. And then perhaps I would be able to impress you and keep you, who it turns out was doing the same thing. I spent my energies at the job, fought the traffic home, ate yet another delicious recipe involving ground beef or chicken wings, and went to sleep. The next day, I did it all over again. And then I turn around, and my wife tells me I'm approaching middle age." Carla gave him a laugh, but Allen wasn't finished. "Then, the work weeks slipped by—I wished them away really—and the weekends arrived. Suddenly, I was thirty and I hadn't done any of the things I thought I would do. I had no idea what I wanted to do any more. So much of a man's life is measured in weekends and dreams of what might have been and moments from the past. And it all began with adolescence, and it's all your fault."

"I see." Carla shook her head in disbelief at the convolution of thought. "Well, I don't suppose 'sorry' helps. But listening to you go on like this, and I realize you're just going on—why, I don't know. You sound like your life is a life of misery. Is your life so bad? You almost sound as if your life was and is a living hell." They turned the corner at Ninth Street. There several blocks down was Jimbo's Car Emporium, its huge sign blocked anything beyond from view.

"Yesterday, or maybe last week, I did think it was bad, in a way. But today, walking and talking and just being carefree with you, I don't think so. But Carla, it's been too long between talks and between walks. You know, I realize now that I really love talking with you. That, at least, is something I never could have done before when I was younger—just talk and be open with you. I've heard people say, 'Your teenage years are the happiest years of your life.' Well, I don't know if that's true. I've been there, and all along the way since then, too, and I'm here to tell you, Carla, I think you and I are ready to be very happy now that we're coming up on middle age." Allen hugged Carla about the shoulder.

"Uh huh. Don't pull me into that boat, Mr. Johnson. I'm still in my mid-to-late twenties."

"Oh yeah? And what about me?"

"You're in your early-to-mid thirties."

"I see. Have a seat, honey. I want to tell you about something." Allen pulled Carla down on a bench and pointed to the car dealership down the road. Then he proceeded to tell her about Jimbo, Joey, the frustrations he had been feeling and even, despite the genuine love and tenderness he felt for them, how sometimes his family made him feel penned into a life, a routine that he felt powerless to control. (He did not tell her about Karen.) Carla listened, nodded, and occasionally asked questions, but mostly she just listened. But she had heard it already in his mock-serious monologue about aging, and she told him so. Allen was feeling trapped and frustrated by living the life into which they had settled. She could either go with him where ever he was trying to go, or she could try to force him into a life he would resent (and thus eventually lose him), or she could go ahead and get it over with and leave him. But she didn't want to leave him, and she didn't want to lose him, so she was along for the ride.

After a while, they stood up and began the walk home, which seemed much longer than the walk downtown. Allen felt relieved of the weight of his solitary invisibility but tired from the energy of releasing that weight. Carla now helped carry that weight which (to say nothing of the extra weight within her) made her steps more difficult. When they finally came into the house, John Wesley ran to them and hugged them. Allen's parents sat quietly but expectantly. Carla was quiet, evidently resolved that her husband felt that he must do this thing, yet unsettled at the prospects. When Allen sat at the kitchen table and explained his plan to his parents, his mother had looked distant and a bit bewildered, but his father had nodded understandingly. When Allen finished with, "And who knows, I might even end up here at Evanston Community College," his mother grinned broadly.

Mrs. Johnson gazed lovingly across the table at John Wesley and Carla. "It will be so nice to have you both so close." She blinked slowly with the pleasant thought. Allen's jaw dropped.

"Mom, I'm in the room. Don't you mean three, err, four of us? "

"Of course, dear. Of course." She smiled benignly, and Allen gaped.

Mr. Johnson only nodded in his best Fred MacMurray pose and asked the obvious. "And how will you live while you are out on this little post-graduate lark of yours, Allen?"

"'Post-graduate lark,' huh? I hope that's not all it is. Well, I haven't figured it all out yet. I thought maybe we would see if Carla can find a position near the university, and then we'd get some school loans, and maybe I'd find some part-time work. It'll work out. We'll be okay. We can economize some and maybe get into student housing and . . ." Allen was prattling on trying to convince himself as much as his father, but his father only nodded and frowned, unmoved. Finally, his father raised his hand, as if he were a traffic cop.

"Hold on. Listen, I had a feeling something like this was coming, although I didn't realize it was as serious as all this. Why you want to waste more education on issues anyone else could answer using common sense, I'll never know. Anyway, I spoke with a friend of mine last night, well, actually he's my banker, and I'm in a position where I can help and, furthermore, I'm willing to help you out, if you want. I really kind of thought you might want to open a little business or something, but if you would rather go to school, I won't put any strings on it." Carla was shaking her head no. She didn't want to take their money, but Allen paid no attention.

"Oh, that's great, Dad. Thanks a lot. Isn't that great, honey?" He turned now to Carla.

"No. I mean yes. It's very generous, but . . ." Her head was still shaking in disapproval.

"It certainly is! What a great dad. You're the greatest, Pop," Allen grinned.

And so it was decided. Allen Johnson had one more shot at visibility. He was prepared to take that shot as a graduate student, and then perhaps a full-blown philosopher at a little invisible college somewhere and sit in a musty office filled with all manner of memorabilia and artifacts that would at once baffle and endear the masses. At least this was the image Allen had worked up.

For the next several months, he would sit in the bathtub, steaming water turning his skin pink, and he would daydream about the character he would be—a bit off-beat, but cherished and respected by administration, colleagues, and students alike. He never pictured himself as a Professor Kamew or even as a Dr. Easy Grade, but saw himself in a kind of caricature of the professors he had come to know when he had been a blissfully obscure (and completely invisible) undergraduate. He nurtured the daydream and even identified some of the artifacts he would need to find for his office, rummaging through flea markets or perhaps estate sales. He would need a bountiful supply of dusty books and bookcases that went from floor to ceiling, although the books would need to be arranged in a careful disorder, stacked up partially over the window and even on the floor at the edge of the office. And a desk lamp. Allen would have to find an archaic little desk lamp made of brass instead of relying on gaudy fluorescent lights in the ceiling. It was a reverie that Allen wallowed in, for he felt that, for once, he was actually creating a scenario that he could control. He could dream on in a delicious fantasy, and then he could make his dream come true. And once he had seen his dream come true, he could settle into his own realm of visibility. He could choose the colors and sounds that would define his image.

Devolution

Oh heavenly teachers, how well I see that according to your principles, there are very few crimes on earth.
-Marquis de Sade

The history of people and their constructions is marked and counted by the changes that occur. When we are young, many of the histories of politics that we study in school are counted by the wars that our society has fought. So as children we learn first of the period, from Colonialism to the Revolutionary War, then we go to the War of 1812, then to the Civil War, and so on. In the lives of people, we count by less obvious yet just as remarkable events. People relate their lives by recounting the birth of children or the loss of loved ones or the acquisition or loss of a job. However, if we draw back from the scene, we are likely to see an even more clearly defined picture where lives are marked by personal crises. As an infant, babies discover their separateness from their mother, and a crisis results. Adolescents eventually learn the frustrations of adulthood, and a crisis results. Young adults leave home to forge a life of their own, and a crisis results. There are other crises to mark the progress of life, too, of course, and likely it varies by each person (unless one is a Virgo, of course, since everything is the same for all Virgos).

Each crisis in a life is defined by what the person was, what he or she wanted to be, had to be, or didn't want to be. And the crisis in each case might be described as a kind of critical mass, when all the elements are separated, exposed, raw, and attempting various coalescences, until finally all the elements are broken down and whatever outcome is necessitated by those raw elements and the catalyst of choice occurs. But before that outcome can emerge, the complete breakdown of the previous elements must take place. Even history points this out. Before great societies can rise or fall, they must go through an intense breakdown; only then can history proceed. To be able to change fundamentally, we must have the structures of our lives broken down. In order to resolve, we must first dissolve, both socially and personally.

Such was the inevitable result of Allen Johnson's crisis, as it is with any crisis. He was on the path of a new definition; the elements were in place; the history was there; the opposing force was there. But to be able to see this change, he had still to dissolve the fabric of his existence.

Allen spent the summer preparing for graduate school. He junked the already junked Pinto. He and Carla sold their tiny cottage to a couple just starting out from Terre Haute. The husband was a professional pest exterminator, having been trained and qualified by rigorous examiners on the most efficacious manner in which to spray an empty cabinet to rid it of roaches, and the wife was a professional interior decorator, educated by mail by one of those schools, the name of which she found in a matchbook, whose home office was decorated with brass geese on the wall to demonstrate her expertise. Carla found a position as an elementary school art teacher some twenty miles from the university. Allen took a position as a Teaching Assistant in the philosophy department, with some considerable help from James, the grand old man in the TA section of the offices, and Dr. Easmane, who recalled Allen's rapt attention in his Contemporary Existentialism class, and rapt attention is always to be cultivated.

At the end of the summer, the baby was born and named Julia after Allen's grandmother, whom they had always called affectionately "Moo Moo." Allen was fond of Moo Moo, but deep within him he also knew that Moo Moo had a large supply of money, and it never hurts to cover all the bases. Allen's sister and her husband recently moved to New York for her residency in neurological surgery. The four Johnsons moved into Darlene's old apartment, filling the vacated, cramped apartment. The apartment was near the campus so Allen could walk to his classes, the library, and the daycare center. Actually, The Slum was also available, but neither Allen nor Carla even considered it as a possibility, having grown accustomed to a modicum of cleanliness in their lives.

Allen was happy as could be, at least for a while, and that happiness made Carla happy too, which made John Wesley and Julia happy. Allen decided all was right with the world. When classes began, Allen entered each class he was taking with a zeal he had not known before as an undergraduate. He read and reread each chapter. He even occasionally read passages from the suggested reading lists, although he soon discovered that such behavior was frowned upon by his classmates (most of whom were recent graduates attempting to remain in college a bit longer and live the life of Maynard).

In the introductory survey classes that he was a teaching assistant for, he was less confident, but he was buoyed by the advice of his friend James. He informed Allen that as frightening as it is to teach that first day, if the teacher can manage to terrorize and baffle the students, they would never notice that, in fact, Allen was barely keeping ahead of the students in the readings, and most of his lecture notes were copied verbatim from the teacher's guide to the textbook. Allen also learned to respond to questions that he did not know the answer to (or that he could not for the life of him figure out what was being asked) by responding, "That's a very good question. Why don't you research that and present it to us the next class?" Despite these defenses, there were always a couple of students who knew immediately of Allen's lack of preparation and who took it upon themselves to discredit him and, if possible, belittle him before the class, which made him blush terribly until he realized he could always flunk them. After Allen realized this salient fact, he just grinned at the students' feeble attempts to wrest away his control, meager though it was, and the students understood the grin of power (which had certain similarities to the grin of the grim reaper) and ceased their attempts to deride poor Allen. Some of the young women in Allen's classes would find that lean power and virile wisdom quite attractive and set plans to garner the attention of this wizened college instructor. But when the semester began, Allen hadn't anticipated any of this, and, all in all, he was pleased with his life.

Some things, Allen noticed, had changed since he had been an undergraduate, though he was not so certain the changes were external to him. He noticed that many of the upperclassmen in the philosophy department had a great deal of disrespect for the professors, giving them nicknames that were most unflattering. For example, Professor Gorner, who told very bad puns in class, was addressed to his face sometimes as Professor Groaner, though he considered it a mere mispronunciation. Dr. Larsen, a very large woman who specialized in nineteenth century English empiricists with red beards and glasses (or something like that), was known as Dr. Large Ass. And Dr. Richard Head III, well, his family had a long tradition of self-perpetuating abuse.

Another thing that Allen noticed was that many students seemed, well, slovenly. It had been different when he was an undergraduate. Sure, he had worn the same jeans for weeks on end. But to Allen's recollection, his jeans didn't actually give off an odor like the odor that emitted from the long haired student who hung around the coffee shop reading Marx and spouting neo-feminist interpretations of current events (which irritated the other young men at the shop who generally espoused more of a liberal stance than what they practiced, and also irritated the young women, since he was stealing their thunder a bit). And some of the other male students almost never shaved and, since their beards were still a bit sketchy, they looked as if they were trying to revive the image of Yasser Arafat.

As a result of these observations Allen made, he felt just a little above the lowly undergraduates. Because he was older than most of the other graduate students (to say nothing of having a family to support and of actually having had a position outside of academe), he almost immediately joined James as one of the "old men" of the department. It was a role Allen soon found comfortable and yet in its way difficult to manage.

Because he seemed to have experienced some of the "real world," Allen was a resource for the other graduate students. They would come to him and discuss their financial crises, which were many, and their personal problems, which Allen felt were generally trivial. He would sit and nod and strike a pose of thoughtfulness, holding his chin in his hand and looking off into space, as if contemplating the resolution of their problems, although he was generally daydreaming by then about his life as a philosopher. Occasionally, he would mutter an "I see" or an "Uh huh." If the counselee asked him a question, he would come back to the conversation and respond with a, "Well, how does it look to you?" But as any counselor can tell you, most people already know what they must do or at least what the options are, so Allen rarely actually gave any advice. Nonetheless, he was considered a trusted and valuable confidante for many of the other graduate students. Allen had a penetrating vision, an ability to see the issues and to identify solutions. Allen reveled in the role and the grand sense of visibility he gained from it, and he soon set up his "practice" at Angelo's Bar and Grill, a college watering hole. Allen would come in after his last class at about three in the afternoon and, beer in hand, start holding sessions with the graduate students until it was time to pick up Julia at four-thirty. Allen felt divinely visible. At long last, his dreams seemed to be matching his actions.

Finally, the day came when Allen, having several large mugs of beer too many, let four-thirty sneak into fifteen after five. When he finally swaggered up the steps to the daycare center, his head was light and spinning. Mrs. Foster, the woman who ran the place, told him that Carla had already picked up the baby just moments before. So Allen stumbled

I'm in the Room

back to Angelo's to hold court some more before he went home to prepare his graduate class presentation on the principle of verification in A.J. Ayer. However, when he returned to Angelo's, he found most of the crowd had changed already, and his table had been taken over by a group of theater arts majors who were having a kind of disjointed conversation by using lines from different plays in which they had performed.

"'My boy Joel was a sailor—knew 'em all. He'd set on the porch evenings and tell 'em all by name.'"

"'That boy is just broken up over Skipper's death. You know how poor Skipper died. . .'"

"'What do you want from me, Brother—that I quit school or just drop dead, which!'"

"'So I'm to blame because that lazy hulk has made a drunken loafer of himself? Is that what I came home to listen to?'"

"'Alexandra, I've come to the end of my rope. Somewhere there has to be what I want, too.'"

"'Don't be so modest. You always started too low.'"

And then they all laughed uproariously, but Allen didn't get any of it so he sat at a booth along one wall and ordered yet another beer. After a few minutes, a fellow master's student who sat next to Allen in his Modern Analytical Philosophy graduate class came in and sat at Allen's booth with him. Janine was slender, brunette, and twenty-two years old. Allen had not really noticed her before except that she always disagreed with the professor, but through the considerable influence of his afternoon libations, he noticed now that she was not unattractive if you were into the blue-jeans-and-tee-shirt kind of girl. Janine exuded a bawdy, free-spirit attitude that Allen found refreshing. When she turned her head to order a beer for each of them, her hair flipped which Allen found enjoyable and rather fetching in his ale-enhanced state.

After ordering their beers, she started telling Allen about how upset she was that her roommate, Cheryl, had moved out and how terrible it was going to be to come home to an empty apartment. Her roommate had even taken the cat, which the two of them loved and thought was wonderful company even though it used the carpeting as a litter box, the furniture as scratching posts, and all company as prey. Allen posed and nodded, concentrating to hold the pose through the effect of some eight mugs. Janine poured out her problems to Allen and gulped her beer and ordered another for each of them, although Allen was having trouble keeping up. He was getting full. When she downed the next one and was ordering another, Allen held up his wobbly hand to say he had had enough. He felt very woozy, but he managed to nod and look concerned and when she finally got to the point of asking, "What in the world am I going to do with all that space?" he was ready with, "Well, what do you think are your options?"

"Let's see," Janine started reflecting on her options as she lifted the mug to drink, and the condensation from the glass dripped water down the front of her shirt startling her into pulling the mug away, which, in turn, caused the beer in the glass to slosh out and down the front of her shirt. Though Allen had seen raunchy wet tee shirt contests back in his undergraduate days, this unintentional private showing was far more surprising. Although Janine pulled the material away from her skin, as soon as she let go of the fabric it clung again to her, and Allen knew immediately that she was braless and chilled. Allen tried not to stare, but his gaze kept returning to the site of the spill. Janine finally could ignore it no longer. "Well, gee, Allen, are you making a mental picture yet?"

"Oh, I'm sorry," Allen slurred. He looked at her face which seemed to be even cuter than he had remembered before, and he couldn't be certain because she was a bit blurry, but he thought she was grinning at his embarrassment. "I'm sorry, Janine," he began again, "it's just that I had never noticed that you even had, that is, in class, I never looked at you as having, well, I never knew you were so pretty." Allen had not really meant to say that, but his gaze and fumbling had gotten the better of him and it seemed a way out. When he looked at Janine now, she wasn't grinning, but had, instead, a sidelong stare.

"Coming from you, Allen, I think I'll take that as quite a compliment. I think you're pretty, too. Maybe I should have poured beer on me before." Janine took a long, pensive swallow of beer putting on her best sultry look, which really wasn't very. Now she leaned forward on the table, resting herself on her arms. "You know, Allen, maybe we should study some together for that class in Analytic Philosophy. Everyone says you're one of the smartest students in the master's program, and some of us think you're pretty cute, too, for a philosophy student." Janine grinned at her joke, then gulped down the rest of her beer very ungenteel-like and readied for another order.

"Shome of the other women think I'm cuhte?" Allen slurred. He thought maybe he liked this visibility with fellow students. His head wagged a bit from the influence of the beer. He tried to glance back at Janine's wet t-shirt, but the beer was beginning to dry. Allen secretly cursed evaporation. Janine saw his attempt to look at her, though.

"Yeah, some of us women. Well, actually a couple of the men, too, but they figured you were off limits, being married and all." Janine smirked as she leaned on the table again, resting on her arms, but this time made certain she shelved the objects of Allen's attention on the tops of her forearms. Allen, with all the subtlety of a construction worker, smiled appreciatively while he stared with blood-shot eyes at her shirt, and Janine gave him a laugh that seemed to say, "I see you." Allen wavered, his head spinning.

The waiter came over to take Janine's order, but instead she raised a finger. "I know," she said too brightly as if she had had the first thought ever, "why don't we get a six-pack and I'll show you all that space in my apartment that I'm talking about and we won't have to spend all our money in here." She chuckled out loud at the transparency of her ruse, but Allen was far too drunk to catch it. She pulled Allen's hand, left some bills on the table, and they left the bar to the slurring soliloquy of a quite drunk theater arts major.

"'Tomorry and t'morry and t'morry shleeps in this pretty place from day to day to the lasht sibrical of decoded time'—Oh. Shit." And glasses crashed as the newest slayer of Macbeth fell over the table to thunderous applause and a roar of approval from his compatriots.

Before Allen really knew it, he and Janine were jostling across campus, a setting sun making the campus square glow golden on a cool September evening. As they walked and compared notes on the various professors, she paused beside a bench to tie her tennis shoe, and Allen, made brazen and amnesic by the beer and Janine's lack of disapproval, touched her shoulder, pawed it, really, in a soft clubbing motion. When she stood up with a question on her face, he pulled her close and tried to kiss her and she returned the attempt, although the combined inebriety of the two of them made it look more like a wrestling match than romance. But it was, after all, a logical turn of events for someone seeking visibility: visibility in the eyes of a member of the opposite sex. And though Allen was quite drunk, he was sober enough to know he liked the attention he was receiving from this woman, who was at any rate different from his ordinary wife Carla. Oh, Carla. Allen caught himself for just a moment, then pushed the thought out of his spinning mind.

The two of them stood there, grappling awkwardly as if they were not standing in the middle of the campus (Allen did not yet know the extent of his visibility), and they both began to pant. Allen found himself trying to run his hand up Janine's damp, stale-beer smelling t-shirt. At first she moaned slightly, then she pulled back sharply and straightened her shirt. "No, we can't do this, Allen. It's not right." Allen grabbed at her arm, missed, retried, caught her wrist, and emulated (or so he thought he was) something out of a romantic movie by pulling her close to him. She stumbled and fell into him, and they both fell in a whump to the ground, her on top of him, where, undaunted if winded, Allen started kissing her again with his mouth open far too wide. After a moment of slobbering smooches, she pulled back again and looked around her, but with unfocused eyes. "No, please Allen, not here."

It was not lost on Allen, even in his inebriated state, that "not here" did not mean "no," so he staggered upright and pulled her along the direction they had been walking. Then she pulled him along until they were in her mostly empty apartment that reeked of cat, and they tumbled around the living room and into her bedroom. When they had satisfied themselves, Allen and Janine rolled apart, and both of them fell fast asleep.

Allen awoke with a start around midnight and sat straight up in bed. His head was pounding, his tongue was fuzzy, and he had no idea at first where in the world he was. He looked at Janine next to him, and his memory returned. He immediately was filled with a strange mix of satisfaction and utter despair. What had he done? Oh, what had Allen Johnson done? When Janine opened her eyes and rose to look at Allen, the bed clothes slid off her body and Allen realized just how tawdry he felt for his infidelity. But he did not yet know just how much trouble he had caused himself. Janine rolled over and smiled up at Allen.

"Well, good morning, Professor Johnson," she purred as she pulled the sheets up over her. Her breath reeked of beer.

"I have to go." Allen stumbled out of the bed and realizing he was without his clothes felt suddenly embarrassed. He tried to dress quickly, but his clothes were strewn about and he was unfamiliar with his surroundings. He hopped and stumbled about in the dark while Janine watched and giggled at his antics. Allen could not find one shoe and started looking under the furniture. He stepped on dried clumps of cat litter and tripped over piles of old magazines until he finally was attired enough to leave. Janine watched and grinned. "Uh, I'll see you later, Janine." Allen's head was pounding.

"I know. Say hello to your wife, bad boy." Janine stepped out of the bed and slithered toward Allen, leaving her cover behind her. She draped her arms around his neck and kissed him passionately. Allen held the small of her back and started to return the kiss, but he wasn't drunk now, and he opened his eyes wide and pulled away suddenly.

"Oh, no. No." He fumbled with his jumble of clothes he had picked up. "Oh no. I have to go." Allen stumbled across the dark room and fell against the door making an echoing thump down the hallway beyond. "Uh, I guess I'll call you?"

"Don't even start, Allen. I'll see you around campus. Don't worry. I'm not in love with you or anything. Good luck with your presentation on Ayer later today."

Allen looked up sharply. "Presentation? Oh my God, my presentation!" Allen glanced at his wrist now void of his watch. "Oh no! I have a presentation to do in just under ten hours. Oh no!" Allen fumbled with the door latch. Janine tried to slink to the door but stepped on a dried clump of cat litter and ended up hopping the rest of the way to avoid anything else. She opened the door and tried to regain her posture of femme fatale, but the moment was long gone. Allen rushed out into the hallway. "I've got to go get ready for class. My God, I'll never get it done. Aiyee!" Allen scrambled down the hall in a fuzzy panic. Janine stood in the doorway wrapped in a sheet, thinking she perhaps looked like Aphrodite, and watched him leave. When Allen looked back just before he ran out of the apartment building, he could see her posing against the door-face, looking thoroughly amused. "Oh no," he groaned to himself.

At first Allen was stymied as to what he might do, but then he remembered his old friend James, whom he had not really seen much since the first week of classes. Allen ran across campus to James's grungy hole of an apartment and pounded on the door.

"James. James, it's Allen. Open up." James opened the door in his underwear and stood staring at Allen.

"What's wrong, Allen? Where's Carla? Is it the baby? What's up?" He opened the door and let Allen in, his face filled with concern. "What's the matter?"

"I need a favor, James. I need for you to tell Carla that I've been here working on a presentation on Ayer all night." Allen was envisioning how he would present this to his wife. Lying was the only option that he saw. That decision would certainly end up bringing him visibility.

"Why? Where have you been? What have you done? What are talking about?" James stumbled over to the couch, his concern replaced by consternation. "You woke me up at twelve-thirty in the morning on the day we have to have Dr. Groaner sit in on our classes to evaluate us so that I can tell some tale to Carla? What have you been up to?"

"Oh, it was just a little, um, mistake," Allen blinked as if his friend could not see him. "You know, nothing too serious." Allen realized he felt the tiniest inkling of self-satisfaction about his little conquest, although to be honest, it's difficult to say whose conquest it was. Then Allen's eyes opened wider. "Wait a minute. We're being evaluated in class today? What day is it? Oh no. It is today, isn't it? What are we supposed to be covering? I don't have any notes! I have class at eight! I don't have any idea what to say. Where are your notes? Can I see what you're doing?"

James grabbed a stack of loose leaf pages from a desk top and shoved them towards Allen. "Here, we're supposed to talk about Bruner. Don't take these, though. They're my only copy. Now suppose you tell me what you're talking about. Mistake? Just what are you saying?" James was up now and looking as menacing as he could in his baggy underwear at Allen. "Are you saying you've been cheating on Carla?" Allen's sudden start must have told James he guessed right. James leaned in again. "Are you crazy? And you want me to tell lies for you?" James paced now, wringing his hands.

"Hold on. You're the Nietzsche guru. Maybe I'm just being the Übermensch, remember?"

"Oh, grow up, Allen. You're not some undergraduate out on your own for the first time. You're a grown man with kids and everything. And Carla. What about Carla? You know, there aren't many women who would put up with you, much less be as good to you as she is. What is wrong with you?" James scolded.

"What about Carla? Can't you tell her I was here all night? She'll never know and she'll never have to be hurt by it. It's not like I'm having some big affair. It was just a spur of the moment thing. It's not like we're in love or anything. We met in a bar and enjoyed meaningless physical gratification with each other. What of it? I'll probably never see her again," Allen lied as he shrank from James' matronly glare. James stood in front of Allen, his hands on his hips, both to look exasperated and to keep his underwear from falling down, tapping his toe while he waited for the response that would be inadequate regardless of what it was.

"Oh, and that should make it okay? You're so shallow you don't even have to care about who you sleep with?" James threw up his hands. "Who is she? Huh? Does she know that you're married? Does she know you have babies? Who is this sleazy little tramp?" James tapped his toe impatiently. "Huh? I'm waiting!"

"Janine?" Allen offered timidly.

James' eyes grew wide, his face reddened, and a vein on his forehead started throbbing. "Janine! What Janine?"

"You know, Janine . . . in the philosophy department?" Allen scooted sideways along the couch away from James who was standing dangerously close to him.

"Janine Clark? Little, introverted, mouse of a thing, Janine?" James stood over Allen, who had shrunk to the far end of the couch. For just a moment, Allen wondered if they were talking about the same person, but he quickly dismissed his thought. Yes, it was the same Janine. James kept his advance towards Allen. "My Janine? My future fiancée Janine?" James glowered at Allen, his eyes red with rage. "My little shy sweetheart Janine? You've seduced the love of my life? How dare you call me your friend?" James stopped and turned his back to Allen and fell silent for a moment. Allen wrongly felt the threat from James ease.

"Well, I, that is, she kind came onto me, James," he offered as a misplaced kind of inside humor among fellows. "She was all over me, you know?" If he could have nudged James, he would have. "She does have a nice body, though."

"Aaargh!" James spun and threw his fist at Allen, but years of academe had slowed his punch, and Allen managed to avoid the blow by diving off the end of the couch. James lunged again, and Allen dodged again. Allen backed up towards the door. James' eyes were red, and tears streamed down his cheeks.

"She's not your little plaything, dammit. I was going to ask her to marry me, you bastard." James swung wildly at Allen and caught him on the shoulder with the end of a punch that didn't hurt Allen but did throw him off balance for a moment. While he staggered to keep his footing, Allen watched as his enraged former best friend closed his eyes in disbelief and charged directly at Allen. James screamed as he bull rushed Allen. "Aaargh!" Allen regained his footing just in time to sidestep and with just a bit of a push sent James headlong into the front door, completely knocking him out cold. James collapsed to a sitting position against the door.

Allen looked at James who had a large knot already rising on his forehead where he had learned a basic law of physics dealing with mass and inertia. James breathed slowly and moaned slightly, so Allen decided it was time to take his leave before James could regain his legs. He opened the door, and James fell flat on the doorstep. Allen stepped over him and trotted down the sidewalk. When he turned and looked back, James was still lying prone on his front porch, looking defeated and quite nearly nude. Allen looked in his hand and saw that he still had the notes James had given him.

"Oh no," Allen moaned. "What have I done?" Allen tried to shake the image of his friend lying in the doorway out of his head, but shaking his head hurt due to the residual effects of the beer the evening before. Allen shoved the crumpled sheets into his pocket and half walked, half ran to the library.

In the library, Allen photocopied several pages from different textbooks on A.J. Ayer. He highlighted various passages with different colored pens, stapled the sheets together, and ran off towards home. When he arrived, all the lights were on, and Allen knew Carla was awake and waiting for him. He thought up his story as he opened the front door. Carla lay on the couch and she stirred nervously as he stepped into the house.

"Honey? Is that you? I've been worried sick. Are you okay?" Carla sat up on the couch and rubbed her bleary eyes. "Where were you?"

"I'm sorry, honey," Allen lied again. "I was at the library working on that presentation I have to do, and I must have dozed off. I just woke up a little while ago, and I would have called, but I didn't want to wake the baby." Allen hugged Carla, and he felt her relax with relief as he held her. "Let's go to bed, honey. I'm beat."

"You smell like . . ." Allen tensed waiting for Carla to finish,". . . like beer."

Allen sighed. "Yeah, I went by Angelo's after class and had a couple of beers. That's probably what made me drowsy later. I'm sorry about Julia. The time just got away from me. It won't happen again."

"Well, I hope not, Allen. Mrs. Foster charges an extra five dollars if we're late, and we have no money to spare. You shouldn't spend too much on beer either, honey." They walked down the narrow hallway towards their bedroom.

"I don't. Mostly other students buy me beer, and I give them worldly advice." Allen started undressing for bed.

"Be careful some little cute fox doesn't try to steal you away from me, Professor Johnson." Allen felt his heart skip a beat. Carla snuggled close to him as he sat on the bed removing the last articles of clothing. Allen's self-loathing tightened his throat.

"Don't be silly." Allen's voice was tight with anxiety.

"Me? Silly? At least my socks match. Where did you get that blue sock, silly? It looks like it could be a blue knee sock for me. Except, of course, I don't have any blue knee socks. Where'd you get that?" Carla looked up at Allen. He saw not suspicion, but curiosity.

"Oh, I don't know. You must have put it in my drawer some time or another. You know I never really worry about whether my socks match. I guess it was somewhere down in the bottom of my drawer, and I just pulled it on." Allen reached over and turned out the light while Carla frowned and tried her best to remember ever in her life owning a pair of blue knee socks. Allen fell into a fitful sleep. Carla, however, laid in the dark, her eyes fully open.

A few hours later, Allen was up early although very bleary eyed and off to deliver his eight o'clock lecture he had stolen from James. When he arrived at his class, the students were unusually noisy and whispered busily amongst themselves even after Allen had smoothed the wrinkled papers and begun reading the notes. Dr. Groaner slipped unobtrusively in the rear of the room so that only the students in the back and Allen, of course, knew he was there. Allen felt his heart pounding as he prepared to introduce the lesson according to James, but the students weren't ready yet to discuss ethics in a textbook. They wanted to discuss Allen's ethics.

"Mr. Johnson, why were you wrestling with that woman in front of the Chi O house last night?" one girl asked with mock innocence. The class tittered. Dr. Groaner raised his eyebrows and waited for Allen's response as well.

Allen felt the blood rush to his face. "I'm sure I have no idea what you are talking about." He tried to put an air of aloofness into his voice. "Now today, we will discuss . . ."

"Oh, you know what I'm talking about, all right." The young woman was a banana peel; if Allen didn't watch his step, he would slip. "That dark-haired lady you were groping out by the park bench. We all thought maybe you were going to do it right there on the ground." The young woman was vicious, and she had the advantage.

"Whatever you may be talking about doesn't concern today's lesson. Now if we could get back to ethics." Allen could feel the sweat beading up on his brow.

"Well, we are talking about ethics, aren't we? I mean, that co-ed wasn't your wife, was she?"

Allen felt trapped. "She's not a co-ed," he blurted. He stepped squarely on the banana peel. It wasn't the right answer. The students snickered at his faux pas. Dr. Groaner began scribbling in his notebook. Allen felt woozy with frustration and fear and fatigue. "Listen, can we just get back to the lesson?"

"Well, then, who was she? She's not your wife, is she? Did you go to her place or yours? Oh yeah, you couldn't have gone to yours; your wife probably wouldn't understand. Or maybe you have one of those seventies-style open marriages?" The banana girl pressed her advantage. The class was beginning to laugh out loud now, except for one young lady in the front row and, of course, Dr. Groaner.

"Okay, that's enough," Allen finally barked. "Everyone just shut up!" Dr. Groaner shook his head. "We will begin today's lecture with a definition . . ." and Allen proceeded to read word-for-word the notes before him. He kept his head down and avoided any eye contact with the students. Most of the students were too busy trying to understand Allen as he mumbled through the lecture so they could take notes, but the banana girl and a group of cronies around her were still busy giggling and making comments to each other. Allen read the lecture then looked up and saw the clock and realized there was still half the period left. "Uh, are there any questions?" The room was deathly quiet now. "Uh, well, I guess you're dismissed." Dr. Groaner looked at his watch and scribbled on his pad while he shook his head. The students filed out murmuring and still snickering, but Dr. Groaner stayed just outside the door to discuss the pedagogic debacle he had just witnessed. The one girl on the front row who had not laughed stayed behind, and when the other students had left, she approached the very defeated teaching assistant.

"Dr. Johnson?"

"Mr. Johnson. I don't have a doctorate and, for that matter, I doubt I will ever get my master's." Allen shoved the pilfered notes into his battered briefcase he had been so proud of when he had brought it home from the secondhand store. It had seemed the perfect briefcase for a college professor. Now, it seemed merely battered and pathetic.

The girl continued despite Allen's obvious disengagement, "Well, Mr. Johnson, I just wanted to apologize for the way the class acted. Some of us think you're very nice and, well, it just wasn't fair the way they treated you." The young lady moved closer to Allen. "I hope you won't hold it against the entire class because some people are rude." She moved closer to Allen, and he could smell her heavy musky perfume. Allen was frozen with bewilderment. The student was directly in front of him now, and he was backed up to the desk. She looked up into his face with a gaze of adoration then closed her eyes, puckered her lips, and kissed him flush on the lips. Allen responded at first by puckering up, but immediately started to pull away.

"Mr. Johnson, may I . . ." Dr. Groaner stood in the doorway looking very flabbergasted. "Oh, excuse me." Carla was standing next to him, the one blue knee sock in her hand, her mouth agape. Allen pulled away from the co-ed who scurried out the front doorway leaving Allen to respond to the people in the back doorway.

"Dr. Groaner, I mean Gorner, it's not what you think. Carla, it's not what it looks like." Allen rushed towards them, student desks tumbling as he waded through them.

"Well, Mr. Johnson, what I think is you were just kissing one of your students. But that's not what was just happening?"

"That's precisely what it looked like to me." Carla scowled furiously. "But if that's not what it was, suppose you also explain the discussion I heard at the beginning of class. I came over here to tell you I've thought and thought about it and I've never in my life owned any damned blue knee socks, and what's more, since I wash all your damned clothes, I know there never was a pair of damned blue knee socks in my damn house before last damn night. But I guess your students would know more about that than I would. Should I chase her down now and return the sock?" Carla's face was twisted with anger and outrage. She held the limp sock before her. Dr. Groaner was also furious, but he figured his anger could wait. Mrs. Johnson had first dibs on abusing the scoundrel after all.

"Mr. Johnson, make an appointment to see me. Meanwhile, you might want to consider something besides higher education for your life's work. Certainly something besides the teaching of ethics." Dr. Groaner whirled around and walked away superiorly, pretending that he himself had not had a fling with his grading assistant some five years before.

"Dr. Gorner, wait." Allen called out as Dr. Gorner walked on down the hall. Allen followed him as far as the hall until he saw James walking toward him to go to his class. Both of James's eyes were black, and he scowled at Allen before going into the classroom. "Um, hello, James, I have your notes if you'd like to . . ."

"That's okay, Mr. Johnson. I accidently gave you the wrong ones. Those were my notes for last Thursday's class. I don't need them. Carla, how are you?"

"I've been better, James. Were you in on his little party last night, James? Looks like it got out of hand." She leaned forward to look at the knot on James's forehead.

"Oh, so you know. Well, good. Me in on his party? No ma'am. In fact, it turns out he was with my fiancée. And then he came over and beat me up." Allen's mouth dropped open. "And to think, I was the best man at your wedding." James walked into his classroom. The students who had arrived early greeted him with a chorus of "Good morning, sir. How are you?" James told them a joke about his black eyes, and the class laughed appreciatively.

Allen turned slowly to face Carla. She glared at Allen evenly and intently. Allen started to try to say something, anything, to relieve the terrible tension, but Carla raised her hand as if to say, "Don't even consider uttering a single word." Allen stared at the floor, kicking the toes of each shoe with the other like a child caught stealing lollipops from a dime store. Finally, Carla saved him from the silence.

"Allen, I think maybe you have achieved all you ever dreamed of and more, in your own perverse way. I'm going to take the kids and move out. We'll be out by the time you get home. I'll send for the rest of the stuff. Meanwhile, you think real hard about what your dreams are and what you really want. You may or may not get all you want. I don't know. It's too soon to tell. And it depends on what you really want."

"I, uh, Carla . . ." Allen began to stammer.

"No, Allen, you haven't thought it out yet. When you can start a sentence with a word other than 'I', then we'll talk. But there's one thing you should know from the start; you have hurt me and disappointed me more than I will ever be able to say. But that won't keep me from trying to say. You will hear about this again. Bet on it." And with that, she threw the dirty blue knee sock at Allen, turned around quickly, and trotted off down the hall. Just before she pushed open the doors at the end of the hall, she let out a deep sob.

Allen stood there for several minutes watching the path Carla had taken down the hallway. The sock was still draped across his shoulder where it had landed. Then he realized there were at least a half dozen other students sitting around in the hall watching the scene, watching him, staring unabashedly at the hapless but quite visible Allen Johnson. Allen glanced around at their faces and finally yelled at one pimple-faced freshman with a slack jaw and pale eyes.

"Well, what the hell are you gawking at? Huh?" Allen threw the sock at the baffled young man who dodged it as if it had been contaminated by killer germs from some festering cesspool.

"Ssshhh," came from a classroom. Allen slunk past the room and looked up in time to see Dr. Easmane looking back at him as he passed, looking very perturbed by the interruption. Then Allen remembered that he had a presentation to give in Dr. Easmane's class the next hour. Allen glanced at his watch and realized he had maybe half an hour to review his photocopied notes before class. He trudged off to his cubby hole provided to him by the philosophy department and pulled the crumpled pages out of his briefcase that he was growing to detest now. He spread the pages on the tiny desk in his cubicle. By the time the class began, Allen had reread the little patchwork quilt of plagiarized textbooks and felt reasonably confident in his ability to slide this ruse through. He could only pray that no one asked him any questions about Ayer. His knowledge base was very tenuous.

When Allen entered the classroom, the word of his embarrassments (and they were growing by the minute) had preceded him. His classmates looked askance at him as he took his usual seat in the middle part of the back of the room. Janine sat in a far corner, not her usual spot, and did not look up at Allen at all which was a great relief to him. Dr. Easmane, whom Allen still called Dr. Easy Grade, walked in through the doorway in a hushed conversation with Dr. Groaner. They whispered back and forth until finally Dr. Easmane exclaimed more loudly, "And it was the wrong lesson? Oh, my!" That was as close to cursing as members of the philosophy department came. When Dr. Easmane came in, he looked directly at Allen and shook his head in dismay.

"Well, today we have three students giving presentations, Mr. Johnson, Ms. Clark, and Mr. Creppes. Mr. Johnson, since Ayer is the earlier topic, why don't you begin?" Dr. Easy Grade was anything but easy grading to Allen. If anything, Allen thought he was more than a little put out by the whole affair, but Allen braved onward, armed with the insightful knowledge of others and the power of highlighters. He stood up before the class and read the piecemeal presentation, reading loudly, if haltingly, since he was unfamiliar with some of the words being used. When he had finished reading the various notes, he looked up, and the class was staring back at him, quite unsure of what to make of the conflicting view points and variability in language Allen had used. But Dr. Easmane was not looking at him. Dr. Easmane was looking down at the floor, his lips pursed knowingly. The room was deathly quiet for a few moments; then Dr. Easmane spoke slowly and evenly.

"Well, that was quite interesting, Mr. Johnson. Some of the ideas you presented, I couldn't have said better myself." Allen beamed just a little that his ruse would succeed. Dr. Easmane continued, "In fact, some of those ideas I didn't present any better myself, because they were my ideas exactly as I put them down in my textbook on Analytic Philosophy." Allen's chin dropped. "Mr. Johnson, if you are going to plagiarize, at least have the common sense to use something obscure and certainly not to use a textbook written by your own professor!" Allen's face grew very hot very quickly.

How could I have been so stupid, he wondered. His head was whirling now, and the sounds around him of classmates whispering and some snickering seemed surreal, louder than normal. Allen looked to the corner of the room where Janine was sitting, and she was hunched over, her shoulders shaking. Was she crying for him because he had made such a fool of himself? Allen thought he would take some solace in pity, if nothing else. Janine looked up at Allen and he saw that she was laughing quietly, but almost uncontrollably, covering her mouth to keep the guffaws from coming out. When she saw Allen looking at her, she doubled over again, putting her face down on the desk and shaking violently.

Allen looked around the room, but there were no sympathetic eyes to be found. Most of the students were shaking their heads in disgust, but some were giggling loudly at his idiocy. Dr. Easmane rose from his seat and approached Allen, who was frozen at the dais.

"Mr. Johnson, you are dismissed." Allen nodded his head, but he was still frozen in place. "Mr. Johnson, you may go now." Allen stared blankly at his former mentor, now tormentor. "Mr. Johnson! You've failed the class! Leave!"

Allen staggered towards the door, Dr. Easmane's words ringing in his ears. Finally, he darted down the hallway, screaming, "Aiyeeee!"

"Ssshhh," came from the doorways along the hall.

The Crucible

May you lead an interesting life.
-An old Chinese curse

Allen Johnson had finally achieved his dreams, in a manner of speaking. He was supremely visible. No one around campus, it seemed, was ignorant of his twenty-four-hour emergence, the groundwork of which he had spent his entire lifetime laying. But, as with any plans a person makes, the unintended results so very often outweigh the intended results, so that in the end, one is likely to curse the very plans one once embraced with the grip of desperation. Faced with the prospect of living out the life that had come forth, Allen sat for a long time in Angelo's, nursing a cup of coffee and considering his options. In the end, Allen decided that a life of visibility and fame was not entirely unlike a life of notoriety and infamy, and unless he was willing to accept that every aspect of his life before had been nothing to him, he would have to try to retrieve something of his previous life.

At first, Allen wasn't sure what there was to go to and what there was to go back to. And then he thought of Carla and The Slum and "In-A-Gadda-Da-Vida" and the reception at Aunt Donetta's house that even Carla had learned to laugh about. And he remembered John Wesley's first steps in their tiny cottage up north and how he had felt odd about his responsibility for creating those steps. And he recalled finally being able to attend his child's birth and the first cry Julia made in the hospital when she had come into the world, purple and slimy. Allen had become faint from the sight of her and had to receive smelling salts. He thought about how everyone in the family had laughed so much about it and how at first Allen didn't think it was all that funny, but how after a while he too laughed at the ridiculous spectacle he must have presented in the delivery room, his face ashen and his eyes rolling about in their sockets.

And then Allen considered his options. He considered the attraction of Janine and how it had made him feel special to be attractive to that other woman but then remembered the sight of her doubled up with laughter at him. And he mulled over his enjoyment at teaching and the pleasure he received when a concept he remembered having difficulty with when he had first started college finally registered with a student, and Allen could see by the expression in his eyes that he had succeeded. But he also thought about the great horde of students more interested in manipulation and excuses than learning. He thought about his daydream that he had been so carefully nourishing—his office so professorial, his demeanor so knowing yet cavalier, his personage revered and respected. And he recalled the nicknames for his professors, the double standards the professors wallowed in, and the hard, unfulfilled frowns on the faces of the older professors like Dr. Fenster (or Dr. Fence Sitter, as his students referred to him), who had advised Allen at the department semester kickoff picnic that he had spent nearly forty years in academe thinking he was doing philosophy, but then realized he had only been masturbating all that time. (Allen had spewed potato salad all over himself hearing this.) Were these really the foundations of his life he wanted to build upon? Allen decided his life of invisibility had been a cruel kind of deception. Sure, he had been invisible to almost everyone else in the universe, but that did not mean his life had had no substance, no meaning. Allen gulped down his lukewarm coffee and ran across the campus to the tiny apartment he and Carla had made into their home.

When Allen arrived home, Carla had been true to her word: she and John Wesley and Julia were gone. Allen wondered why she was automatically entitled to abscond with his children but realized immediately that he was indeed on shaky ground to raise any sort of ruckus about it just now. On the refrigerator were various colorful mélanges in John Wesley's awkward hand, along with photographs of Julia and a partial grocery list with hamburger meat and chicken wings at the top of the list. There was also a photograph of James, and Allen felt an immediate pang of guilt when he saw it. He had to try to explain his actions to his best friend, but it wouldn't be easy. Finally, there was a note from Carla, informing Allen that she would be staying at a colleague's apartment, one Kelly Braun, and Allen's head grew hot in wonder and fear. Allen called the number on the paper and a man answered and when Allen had stammered, asking to speak with Carla, the man on the other end had put his hand over the phone and spoken to someone before Carla had finally come to the phone.

"Hello, Allen. What do you want?" Carla's voice was low and unwavering.

"Carla, you were right to be so angry with me."

"That's not news. What is it you want to say, Allen?"

Allen was stumbling. He pictured his wife leaving him for some elementary school teacher named Kelly whom his kids would learn to call "Daddy".

"Carla, we need to talk. Will you see me?"

"Yes, Allen, I will. Come on over. The directions are on the back of the piece of paper with the phone number on it. I'll see you soon. Oh, and Allen?"

"Yes?" Allen felt utterly at Carla's mercy.

"Change your clothes." The line went dead.

Allen looked at the clock and saw that it was three now. He flipped the piece of paper over and saw that the address was one of those single's apartment buildings on the outskirts of town, some twenty minutes from the university, but generally very popular with the moneyed upperclassmen. Allen felt his heart sink. It was awfully fast, he thought. Carla must have had this Kelly Richboy Braun on the line to be able to move right in the first time Allen messed up. Why, she was probably just as guilty, no, more so, as Allen. She'd probably been having a big fling with this Kelly Sugar-Daddy all along; it was just that Allen was the one that got caught. Allen felt a righteous indignation come over him. Then he glanced at the refrigerator and saw James's picture. First things first, Allen thought.

Allen knocked on James's door with a careful rap. He had considered how to approach James all the way over to his apartment. He couldn't decide whether to blurt out the whole sordid truth, how he had flirted with Janine and she had flirted back, and he had quite consciously decided to sleep with her about as consciously as she had decided to sleep with him, and how it had been a brief, flippant thing, but not, in the end, a capital offense. It was not, after all, as if they had been consorting about for months, laughing at James's and Carla's ignorance while the two of them debauched. Or, perhaps that was too direct. Perhaps he should be more circumspect, couching his terms in muted tones so that James might feel less anger at Janine, who was to be, after all, James's wife. It could easily be argued that both Allen and Janine were under the influence of too much beer and too much stress from graduate school and the strident financial circumstances that situation presents. It was a human sin, wasn't it, and humans aren't perfect. And if James could just see that Allen was truly sorry for the betrayal James must be feeling (although, again, it wasn't any really big deal— no, he probably should leave that part out. It clearly was a big deal to James).

"Well, what do you want?" Allen was startled back to the present by James's face, looking so much like a raccoon with the two black eyes that Allen was immediately amused, although his common sense, such as it was, prevailed and he did not laugh. "Janine, I think it's for you." James turned and walked back into the apartment. On the couch, Janine was sitting very still, her face red and streaked with tears. "Well, come on in, Allen. We're just one big happy family here, aren't we?" James's voice was heavy with sarcasm. Allen stepped into the apartment and closed the door. "Well, Allen, did you come here to pick up Janine? You two have a date tonight as well?" James threw his hands up in disgust.

"James, listen. . ." Allen tried to choose which path to take.

"Well, I guess I'd better listen if Allen says listen, though God knows I don't suppose he can give me any more black eyes for a while." James shrugged.

"Okay, now stop it." Allen surprised himself and James as well. "Now you and I both know that I didn't intentionally hurt you last night."

"Oh, well now, let's talk about intentions . . ."

"Now just stop it, James, and let me finish. I'm withdrawing from the college and I've given up my assistantship." James turned and looked at him in disbelief. "Oh, it's not because of last night. Or it is and it isn't. I don't think I'm cut out for the college life. I probably never was, but that's not why I came over here. Listen, what happened last night between me and Janine was a juvenile and stupid mistake. We're both old enough to know better, and I especially should have known better, being married and all. But it's not the end of the world. If you and Janine have something good together, then you should work through this. If not, it's better to find out now than later." James stood still, considering Allen's words. "Besides, we've been friends for far too long to leave it like this. If you want to stay angry at me, fine. I'll be out of here and I'll never bother you again. But if you want us to try to hang onto some form of our friendship, then we can. It's your call. But whatever happens between you and Janine, you should know that it was not strictly my fault. I'm not that important. And come to think of it, I'd rather not be that important."

Janine spoke for the first time since Allen had come in, her voice defensive but steady, "Well, you weren't exactly innocent. You practically threw yourself at me out on the mall." James's eyes showed mounting confusion.

"No, Janine, neither one of us was innocent. I do believe our actions last night were quite mutual. And we both carry some of the blame. True, I think I carry more blame, but this can't be about me."

"I guess we were both, um, consenting." Janine looked at the floor. "But, you know, I think maybe he's right, James." She turned and looked up at James who looked very alone just then. "I mean about you and me. I don't think I'm ready to be tied down to just one fellow yet, even if it's someone as wonderful as you. I guess I just kind of felt a little trapped. We were getting so serious, and I knew you were thinking long term and I guess something inside of me just leaped at a chance to do something else. I feel so, so dirty now." Allen thought about how that made him the carrier of dirt and he wasn't sure he liked the sound of that, but he said nothing. "I'm truly sorry I hurt you, James."

"I don't know." James shook his head. "Maybe you're both right. I'll have to think about it all. But you'll never know how much I feel for you, Janine. And a part of me will always go with you when you leave here. But perhaps you're right. Perhaps I did want too much too fast."

"It will all work out, James. You'll see." Janine stood and caressed his swollen cheeks. "And you'll always be my special philosophy raccoon, James." Allen sputtered with a sudden laugh.

James looked quickly at Allen. "Don't push it, Johnson."

"Uh, right. Sorry, I'll just be going." Allen walked towards the door.

James followed, "Listen, Allen. You don't have to give up your assistantship. I'll talk to Dr. Easmane and we'll . . ."

Allen stopped on the sidewalk. "No, James. I don't want to talk to Dr. Easmane or Dr. Gorner and anyone else for that matter. The truth is, that vision of myself was built on false premises. I'm not the person who can become what I thought I wanted to become. I'll be fine. But I've got to go. I've got to try to fix things up with Carla. I know what's important to me now." Allen turned and walked away down the sidewalk.

"Good luck, Allen. I'll see you later," James called from the door. Allen rather liked the sound of that and allowed himself a small smile.

Allen took the bus out to the address on the little slip of paper and searched the doors for the apartment of Kelly Wife-Stealer Braun. When he reached the right door, he knocked loudly. He could hear the children, his children, inside playing.

"Yes?" A young woman opened the door and peered out at Allen.

"Is this Kelly Braun's apartment?" Allen was ready for a fight.

"Yes. I'm Kelly Braun," the young woman looked out fearfully, as if Allen were an insurance salesman. Allen felt a wave of relief and, yet, a letdown. He had been geared for a confrontation for no reason. "You're Kelly Braun?"

The Crucible

"Yes. Who are you?" She replied, mildly annoyed now.

"I'm Allen Johnson. Is Carla here?" Allen tried peering into the apartment.

"Check his socks first." Carla spoke from somewhere in the room. Kelly started to look down at Allen's feet. Allen pushed closer to the door until he could see Carla sitting on the couch.

"Carla? We need to talk." Kelly kept her foot on the door, just in case Allen really did try to push past her. "Please tell your friend to let me in."

"Let him in, Kelly. But don't stand too close. He's scum, you know." Kelly stepped aside and watched Allen enter the room. She grimaced as if she had taken a bite of something disgusting as Allen passed. Allen rolled his eyes and went over to Carla. John Wesley and the baby played on the floor, oblivious to the tension between Allen and Carla. Carla did not look at Allen. Allen sat on the end of the couch, Carla looking over the back of the couch and out the window at nothing.

"Um, when I called earlier, some man answered . . ." Allen looked questioningly at Kelly. Carla couldn't help but smirk.

"That was my brother." Kelly said it with such an air of "you stupid idiot" that Allen immediately felt ridiculous for the sordid scene he had painted in his head of his wife fooling around. Kelly turned and shook her head in disbelief as she left the room. Allen turned his attention to Carla.

"Carla, you have every right to be mad at me." Allen started. His hands were moist, his throat tight. "You are the only woman I have ever loved." Carla sat unmoved, with only a brief snort to acknowledge that Allen was speaking. "What I did was inexcusable and wrong. I know that. I'm truly sorry. In fact, I guess I'm about the sorriest fellow around. You don't know the whole story yet, though." Carla's eyes narrowed. "No, no, not that. I mean that I've given up my teaching job. You were right; I don't have the patience for teaching." Carla was only slightly moved, but she did manage a look of "I told you so." "Also, I've withdrawn from the graduate program." Allen wrung his hands. Carla turned and looked at Allen now for the first time since he had come into the room. "I know that I betrayed your trust and our marriage." Allen groveled on. Carla looked at him pityingly. "If you will let me, I will try my best to earn your trust again." John Wesley came over and sat in Allen's lap. The baby kicked on the floor. Carla's face told Allen her hard stance melted just a touch.

"Why did you do that?" she finally asked. "No, I don't even want to know. I can't imagine what was going on in your pitiful, male head. But tell me something, and tell me the truth. Have there been others?"

"What? No, of course not. What kind of fellow . . ." Allen trailed off.

"No, honey, there haven't been any others and there never will. I swear. It was a one-time sin, I promise." Allen held his hand up Boy Scout-style.

"Well, for the kids' sake . . ."

Allen jumped up, lifting John Wesley up on his shoulder. "Oh Carla, you won't be sorry. I've learned some big, no, huge lessons from all this. You're gonna see a whole new Allen Johnson."

"I'd rather see the Allen Johnson I married." Carla stood up too and picked up the baby who was starting to fuss a bit.

"No, Carla, that Allen Johnson was on the wrong track. I know now what it is I need to do." Carla rolled her eyes as if to say "Here we go again," but Allen turned and looked at her solemnly. "Carla, I wasn't happy as a youth because I was always wishing I was someone or something other than what I was. I've continued that throughout my life. But now I know that what I was, where I came from, who I was, all those things were fine, but I just didn't realize it. Come on; let's go home. Kelly?" Kelly stepped out from the bedroom where she had been obviously eavesdropping and gave Allen a disdainful glare. "Kelly, thank you for being such a good friend to Carla and for taking care of my family today. We will think of you often. You're a fine person. Now, let's get out of here." And Allen and Carla and John Wesley and Julia Johnson went back to their home near the campus.

After a few weeks, Allen and Carla were able to get back on more even footing, though she found it difficult to say "yes" to his nocturnal overtures for quite a while. Otherwise, they resumed a normal, albeit a new normal, lifestyle. Carla finished out the year at the elementary school while Allen tended bar at Angelo's. After a while, the students and faculty who came in forgot about Allen's day of ignominy, or another scandal grabbed their attention, and before long James came in and even Janine occasionally, although Allen never quite forgot how she looked in the doorway that night or in class the next day. He always assumed a friendly but distant demeanor when he had to wait on her table.

And once, the president of the alumni association, Karen Dobroski, came in and, seeing Allen, she had raised her eyebrows and clapped her hands. "Well, well, Allen Johnson, isn't it? And holding down a job, I see." And she had leaned forward familiarly on the bar. "I am so proud of you! Weren't you interested in going to graduate school, or something? That's right, philosophy! You know, I have some pull with the administration, if you want to leave this very nice but, let's face it, dead-end job. Not that you need to return to the streets or anything." She held her hands out in a stop motion.

The Crucible

"Listen, Karen," Allen interrupted, "I told you before. I'm not a street person. And I don't want anything to do with philosophy!" Allen walked away. Karen sat very quietly for a few minutes, blinking her eyes in confusion, then shrugged and left. Allen sighed a huge sigh of relief.

Kelly Braun came over for dinner with the Johnsons sometimes, which at first served to remind Allen that his road back to total acceptance was a long one, but later was designed to match-make her with James, which actually worked out very nicely and years later, after James surprised everyone and received his doctorate, they were married and had five kids, none of them named Allen.

The next summer, Allen and Carla Johnson took their family back to Evanston to visit Allen's parents whom John Wesley called Gramps and Granny. Of course, Gramps and Granny never knew all the details about Allen's self-destruction in graduate school, but they knew he had messed up royally. They were delighted, however, when Allen and Carla informed them that they were moving back so that Carla could take a position as head of the art program in the Evanston school system. It was only later that summer when they were searching for a place to live that Allen saw the ad in the paper:

FOR SALE -
General Store with Gas Pumps.
3 BR Owner's Qrtrs. 20 min. Evanston. Owner Financing.

Allen spread the paper before Carla. "Carla, I know this store."
"Uh huh." Carla looked suspicious.
"This is it. I need to talk to the lady that owns this. Will you go with me?"
Carla saw the resolve in Allen's eyes. "Okay, we'll go. But we're just going to talk."

Allen drove the back way to Okra Cash and Carry, missing only the turn off the River Road, but he quickly realized his mistake and back tracked. Carla was hopelessly lost. When they pulled up, the building had been freshly painted by Jimbo's lot boys and even the inside smelled of fresh paint. Carla approached the store cautiously, but Allen leaped up the steps and pulled open the screen door with the Colonial Bread sign and stood beaming in the little store. Mrs. Fuller sat rocking behind the counter (although she still did not have a rocking chair). The shelves were still sparsely stocked, but the store was immaculately clean. Allen ran back to the door to help Carla with the baby. As soon as Carla entered the store, she had to admit she felt at home. She looked around at the fading signs and the rounded Coca-Cola coolers from a bygone era and she couldn't help but grin. Allen walked slowly up to the counter.

"Ma'am?"

"Yes? Oh, I'm sorry," the woman started. "I must have gotten lost in a daydream."

"Yes, that's easy to do." Allen nodded knowingly.

"Well, can I help you young'uns?"

"Yes, ma'am." Allen rubbed his hands excitedly. "You can sell me your store." Carla spun around to look at Allen, who was fairly hopping with excitement.

"Well, I could do that. My boy Jimbo wants me to move into town with him, so I'm bound to sell I guess. Lemme show you 'round." The woman rose with some difficulty.

"Can I help you?" Allen reached across the counter to keep the old woman from losing her balance.

"Thanks. I'm moving a mite slowly these days. Broke my hip back in the fall. Fishin' for catfish over in the river yonder. You know that River Road?"

"Yes ma'am." Allen looked at Carla. "I fished right there where the road from the sycamore grove comes out." The woman looked up at Allen, surprised.

"You a local boy? You look a tad familiar, but I cain't says I recall you. You old man Waller's boy? Naw, he's older'n you."

"No ma'am, I'm from Evanston. I've fished with you, though, right there on the bank of that river just last year." Allen looked at her for a sign of recognition. The old woman pondered on it, then her eyes opened in recollection.

"Oh yeah, I think I do recall. You're dat boy who gave me the fish. You sure were catchin' 'em. As I recall, I acted a bit testy 'cause I weren't catchin' nothin'"

"Well, I was having some beginner's luck."

"That's all right, son." Mrs. Fuller turned and started toward the back door. "You done okay." The old woman showed Carla and Allen every corner of the store and then she took them upstairs to the apartment that was sparse, clean, and heavy with the odor of sachet. The apartment was surprisingly large, running the length of the store, and Carla started to grow excited about the space and the possibilities. Then they toured the three acres of land, and Carla discovered a wonderful outbuilding to put a kiln in. It was clear that Carla and Allen were growing attached. The two of them huddled with John Wesley and Julia in the old barn.

"Carla," Allen held her hands, "this is home." Carla shifted nervously.

"It's not exactly the place for you to find fame and fortune, Allen. Do you really think you'd be happy here?"

"Carla, one of the things I've discovered by being a total idiot is that visibility is only for the very strong, and I'm not ready nor am I willing to go through the pain and give up the life we have for it. What I want to do is buy this little store and we can sell pottery you make, and we'll get some chickens if we want, and we'll live happily ever after. We'll make a flying leap to happiness."

"You know what, Allen?" Carla blinked back a tiny little tear. "I can see it. For the first time, I can see it."

So Carla and Allen bought the old Okra Cash and Carry (the old woman financed it for less than their rent up in the city had been. They would have plenty from Carla's job to pay for the store and buy clay).

The woman asked for two weeks to clear her things out, and Carla and Allen spent those two weeks gleefully packing to move to the tiny burg of Okra, Kentucky, twenty miles up the river from Granny and Gramps, who were elated when the kids told them.

"We can't wait to spoil those babies, you know," Roger Johnson told them.

"And we are always available to babysit," Jean said, which made her husband start a bit, but then he too grinned at the thought.

"Dad? Will you say it to me, one more time?"

"You've got this Son. You don't need my help."

Carla looked between them as if a ping pong match were being played. "Please, Dad?"

Roger Johnson shook Allen's hand and said, "Give it a ride, Son." Allen beamed.

When Allen, Carla, and the children returned to their new home two weeks later, all their worldly possessions piled in the back of a U-Haul trailer, Mrs. Fuller was just getting into one of Jimbo's long, black town cars.

"Well, kids, it's all yours. Key's on the peg by the back door." The old woman looked wistfully at the old store. "I spent fifty years in that store. Married. Raised young'uns. She's like one of my family."

"Well, Mrs. Fuller, I hope you'll come back often and visit us. We'd like that very much." Carla shook the woman's trembling hand.

"We'll take good care of it, Mrs. Fuller." Allen waved from the step to the porch.

"Come here, boy, there's something I need to tell you." She sounded vaguely menacing and Allen stepped forward timidly. "If'n you an' yours have made up your minds that this is the place you wanna live," the old woman shook her finger at Allen, "then I figure you've probably been down more'n one road gettin' here."

"Yes, ma'am, I guess I have."

"Yes, I guess you have." The woman waved the driver on. She looked through the window at Allen and gave him a smirk. "I can see right through you, son."

"Yeah, I know," Allen grinned and waved as the car started off. "Ain't it great?"

Epilogue

I seem to be a verb.

-R. Buckminster Fuller

When Allen Johnson took his leap, he did not land anywhere. That is the nature of such actions. Instead, what he embraced was not the landing at all, but the leap itself. Now Allen had no way of telling if he was flying or falling, having no frame of reference for either possibility, but he knew it didn't matter which he was doing. All that mattered was that he was in motion. That much he could feel as surely as he could feel hunger or fullness, anger or sadness. It was a new becoming, and it was a becoming he could revel in.

CPSIA information can be obtained
at www.ICGtesting.com
Printed in the USA
LVOW07s2333021116
511444LV00006B/170/P

9 781940 771243